THERE WILL BE ONE

THE WINDSHINE CHRONICLES, BOOK 2

TODD SULLIVAN

MOCHA MEMOIRS PRESS

THERE WILL BE ONE

THE WINDSHINE CHRONICLES, BOOK 2

By Todd Sullivan

MOCHA MEMOIRS PRESS

Rock Hill, SC

OTHER MOCHA MEMOIRS FANTASY TITLES

Other Mocha Memoirs <u>Fantasy</u> titles

Hollow Men: The Windshine Chronicles by Todd Sullivan

Mutiny on the Moonbeam by Rie Sheridan Rose

The Soul Cages by Nicole Givens Kurtz

The Portal Guards by Marcia Colette

Moses: The Chronicles of Harriet Tubman by Balogun

To my parents, with love. —Todd

W oo Jin had been trained to kill opponents in
honorable combat, so the government official's
assignment made his stomach clench.

Assassination.

In a wooden pavilion at the foot of an oreum, one of
the many small mountains dotting Jeju Island, Woo Jin
stood with his hands at his sides, back straight, sweat
trickling down his neck. Official Yeo watched him. The
whirling buzz of mosquitoes and the sharp cries of birds
punctuated the heavy crickets' drone.

"The foreigner's death must happen far from the
island," Official Yeo said. He sat at ease, a long black
pipe between his slender fingers, his arm draped over
the back of the low bench. "It must not be traced back
to us."

A breeze rustled the official's hanbok, a light blue
shirt and silk pants. From beneath the wide, bamboo
brim of the black hat perched on his head, he regarded

Woo Jin. Then he reached down to a leather pack at his feet and removed a bow and narrow wooden case. He presented them to Woo Jin, who accepted the items with both hands.

Woo Jin undid the clasp of the case and gasped. Two dozen pyeonjeons! He'd heard of the short arrows, but he'd never actually seen them before. Known for their incredible boring strength, a pyeonjeon could pierce any armor if shot by an expert archer. Their craftsmanship was a secret heavily guarded by a handful of fletchers in South Hanguk, their deadliness and accuracy as renown on the battlefield as the distinctive whistle of their passage when fired from a bow.

"Coat the tips with this venom." The official produced a porcelain bottle from the folds of his hanbok. "It works quickly, and the antidote is known only to a few specialists. If you attack the foreigner far from populated areas, no one should be able to help her."

Woo Jin's gaze swept over the weapons. He knew he shouldn't question a superior, but the words scorched his mouth and spilled from his lips.

"But why me, sir?"

Official Yeo's eyes hardened. Woo Jin's hands trembled, the arrows in the case knocking against each other. He averted his gaze as he waited for the reprimand.

"You are sixteen now. Yes?"

Not trusting himself to speak, Woo Jin nodded.

"When you're young, the future seems far away," Official Yeo said. "There always seems to be enough time to accomplish all your desires. But when you become an adult, you discover that time is finite and slips through your grasp like grains of sand." Official Yeo lifted his palm and spread his fingers. "Soon, your parents will match you with a young woman to marry. You will have children. Your responsibilities will grow, and time will slip away even faster. Your thoughts will settle, as the minds of all married men, into a place and a routine. Aspirations of grandeur become eroded by responsibilities and practical daily concerns. The fire burning inside of men becomes smothered by the daily grind. Eventually, the flames die. Before this happens, you *must* make a name for yourself. You *must* become a hero while you are young, for it will not happen when you are old."

Woo Jin didn't want to tempt the official's wrath further by disagreeing with him, so he bowed. "I thank you for your wisdom, sir," he said, his voice calm despite the turmoil of his thoughts. "I will do as instructed."

A moment of silence passed. Woo Jin couldn't see the official's face from his lowered position.

"Go now and get ready. Tomorrow morning you will meet your fellow companions. No matter what you discuss amongst each other, you must tell no one your true mission. If your task is discovered, you will never be able to return to the island, even if you survive the coming quest. Do you understand?"

Woo Jin swallowed in a throat gone parched. "I understand," he croaked. "I will tell no one else." Rivulets of sweat snaked down his cheeks to the tip of his nose and plopped to the wooden planks below him. He didn't look up, would not meet the official's gaze. After a while, he heard the man stand.

"You have been spoken highly of by the people of the island. I see that their praise is well deserved. You will attain great rewards in this world, Woo Jin."

"Thank you, sir."

Woo Jin listened as the official went down the pavilion's steps. He didn't raise his head until many moments had passed. When he dared stand up from his low bow, Official Yeo had disappeared down the narrow trail running through the trees. He had left the leather bag behind, so Woo Jin repacked the pyeon-jeons and bow in the case and slung it over his shoulder. He went in the opposite direction of the official, passing farms and rice paddies until he reached his village's perimeter. Round homes made of black volcanic stone with thatch roofs mushroomed up behind the spiked gates. Villagers bowed to Woo Jin as he walked past. Normally, he held his head high and greeted them with cheer. Today, the humidity closed in around him and made his movements sluggish. He called out half-heartedly to elders, giving them lopsided smiles.

He reached home. His father stood in an open schoolhouse, a dozen pupils seated on the floor before him. The students had formed a semicircle around a thick book of bamboo pages filled with tiny script and were bent close over the text in study. As Woo Jin approached, one of the boys looked up and shouted his name. The others followed suit, but a thunderous look of disapproval from Woo Jin's father silenced them.

"Continue reading," his father instructed, then turned to Woo Jin. "The horse has arrived to take you to the city. Your supplies have been prepared." He eyed the bag Woo Jin carried. "You will spend the night in Jeju-si so that you will be rested and prepared to meet the governor early tomorrow morning."

Woo Jin kept his voice low. "Appa, we must speak." He glanced at the students behind him. "Can we go somewhere private?"

The most educated man on this side of the island, Woo Jin's father had piercing black eyes and an inexhaustible appetite for knowledge. Yet he didn't seem interested in joining him, which surprised Woo Jin. He had gone to the meeting empty handed and returned carrying a leather pack that did not belong to him. Why wasn't his father curious about it?

"Appa, it will only take a moment," he said. "I must discuss what the official revealed to me."

"Why? If the conversation was meant for the three of us, I would have been invited to join you."

"Appa," Woo Jin pleaded.

His father glanced over his shoulder at the students studying behind them. "Quickly, then," he said. "Follow me."

They walked back down the village road, out of the gates and entered the trees. They took a narrow path to the nearest oreum. Woo Jin had hiked this mountain many times during his childhood. When he was younger, he had found the sharp ascent up the twisting trail exhausting. Now he went up effortlessly beside his father, the air cooling as they climbed up high above the forest floor. The trees broke away at the apex of the oreum. The eternal Jeju breeze brushed against their faces and played in their hair. The wide blue sea stretched as far as the eye could see and fell off into the horizon.

Woo Jin waited for his father to begin speaking. Moments passed in silence, his father staring out across the island.

"Appa." Woo Jin unslung the pack from his shoulder and set it at his feet. "I must tell you what Official Yeo requested me to do."

"Must you?"

His father didn't turn to him as Woo Jin undid the pack and took out the bow and quiver.

"These weapons." Woo Jin held them up. "Official Yeo gave them to me."

His father glanced at them, his eyes narrowing. "Nothing is *given*. Nothing is *free*."

"But these were, appa," Woo Jin insisted. "I did not ask for this. I did not pay for them."

His father guffawed and cast his gaze back out at the surrounding waters. "You didn't ask for them, and you didn't pay for them, yet there they are in your possession. Perhaps this is the doing of the ancestral spirits? Perhaps they met with the official beforehand and procured these weapons for you?"

"Appa?" Woo Jin shook his head in confusion. "The official wants me to use these weapons, and I must tell you why. I must tell you who he requested that I use them on."

He swallowed. Now that the moment had come, he

struggled to speak the words out loud. He felt tainted just thinking about it, yet there had to be a mistake. Once he told his father, his father would take over from there. He would send a message to the governor's official and explain that his son fought with honor, that Woo Jin wouldn't shoot an opponent in the back with an arrow coated with poison. Especially against a person who lived amongst them on the island. The foreigner didn't mingle with Jeju people, but she deserved a fair chance to fight back against someone trying to kill her. No one should be cut down before they were given the opportunity to defend themselves.

"I am supposed to," Woo Jin paused, "use this weapon against the foreigner."

He waited for the display of shock and disgust on his father's face, but his father remained impassive. Woo Jin realized that he must not have quite understood his meaning.

"Appa." Woo Jin spoke slowly to give each word the weight he knew they deserved. "Official Yeo has requested that *I kill the Dark Elf, Windshine.*" Even though they were alone, he spoke the last words in a hushed voice and glanced over his shoulder at the trees behind them.

After several moments, his father stirred.

"My son," he said, enunciating each word, "you are a fool."

Woo Jin gasped. "Appa!"

"But you are young," his father continued, "and the young hold idealistic notions of the world in heads untouched by the realities of life."

Woo Jin shrank from his father, who stood tall and resolute as he gazed down upon him.

"You have never left this island. Indeed, you've only infrequently left our village. You have spent your youth in study of the mind and the body. It has cost a fortune to create the person standing before me now, but I spared no expense this time, for have I not already lost two sons? Had I prepared them better, would they still be here amongst the living?"

His father motioned to the wide waters surrounding the island. "I have done all I can for you. I am convinced you are a capable fighter, though you will find battle very different from practice in the dojang. Your instructors know this and have prepared you for that moment when you must slay the person trying to slay you. They have spoken highly of you, and they are paid handsomely not to lie. They *do* know the dangers of combat and stake their reputation on the success of their students. Your instructors say you will show great bravery and courage in the heat of battle, and so I believe you will.

"But my son, the world of man is complicated. Being the best doesn't mean you gain the ultimate prize. There is luck and providence to contend with. If these are not in your favor, you will lose. Sometimes the weakest stands last amongst the strong purely out of coincidence. Life is not fair. The struggle to become someone, to be more than your peers, does not come without incredible obstacles and hardships. Not everyone is meant to be a hero."

Woo Jin had never heard him speak thus. Had his

father always thought this way, or had it happened after the death of Woo Jin's older brothers? That had been years ago. Woo Jin didn't remember his father grieving as his mother had. His father had been emotionless as his brothers were buried in the family mounds.

But had he been grieving in his own way? Was that why he spoke these harsh words today, the lack of warmth in his lecture chilling the space between them?

"You shouldn't think too much about the foreigner, as there's much you do not understand about her role in the lives of South Hanguk people. Remember always that not everything is as it seems. There have been many discussions about her and her influence upon the governor of Jeju. Discussions that need not concern you now."

Woo Jin avoided his father's eyes. The points he made seemed crafted to convince Woo Jin that this assassination must be carried out for the good of Jeju people. Yet what about honor?

"To kill a woman who has done me no harm," Woo Jin said, his tone moderated so as not to seem disobedient. "Even a foreign woman like the Dark Elf. I do not know if I can do this, appa. It does not feel right."

His father rested a heavy hand on his shoulder. "You do not understand enough to determine right from wrong. Leave that to the elders, with wisdom and experience."

When Woo Jin still hesitated, his father's grip tightened on his shoulder. "You must do this, my son. This request has already been given to you. The plan has been revealed. There are powerful men within Jeju's government who have gambled much on you completing this commission. If you refuse, they will have no choice but to silence you so that you will not reveal the secret to anyone else. And as I now also know the plan, they will kill me alongside you."

For a moment, Jeju's eternal breeze stilled, its breath, too, caught in surprise at the revelation. The world around Woo Jin froze, the horror of his father's last words working their way into him like the poison he had been instructed to use against the foreigner.

Surely people were not so cruel? Yet nothing changed in his father's expression to leave Woo Jin with any comfort other than that his failure would lead in the death of them both.

2

The horror of the revelation rocked Woo Jin, his heart contracting painfully and bile filling his mouth. Sunlight turned the green of the oreum garish, forcing Woo Jin to squint against the glare. Jeju's eternal breeze restarted with unusual strength, tearing at his clothes and threatening to knock him off his feet.

His family were islanders. They belonged to Jeju. Official Yeo and the cabal that had crafted the plan to assassinate the foreigner wouldn't really threaten them? Woo Jin thought of his younger siblings and his mother. If he revealed the murder plot to others, he may be putting them all in danger.

"You must leave now, Woo Jin. Your belongings have been packed, and the hostler is waiting with your horse."

His father started back down the oreum without another word. Woo Jin watched him enter the surrounding trees and had to exert tremendous effort to move his feet to follow. He stumbled along the trail leading down the mountain. He struggled to breathe, sweat trickling down his face into his shirt. The descent seemed to take hours. When they walked back through the spiked gates, Woo Jin barely registered the village around him. He couldn't distinguish words in the voices that addressed him. People opened their mouths wide and brayed, and Woo Jin stared wide-eyed as he trudged forward on wooden feet.

His vision only cleared when they reached home and he saw his mother. She wore a simple hanbok with a pink shirt and green dress. She smiled, but as he neared, her bright greeting fell away to be replaced by concern. She glanced at his father a few steps ahead of him. Woo Jin wished his mother would come and wrap her arms around him. It would help keep him on his feet. She used to do that when he was a child and exhausted after long hours of practice at the dojang. She would have cool water for him to drink, and tuna kimbap to replenish his strength.

Today, though, she stood her ground. Clasping her hands in front of her, his mother said, "Everything is prepared. On this day, you leave the village as a man to claim glory."

The students at the school cheered Woo Jin's name. His father stood to his right, and a growing crowd of villagers gathered to watch him depart. He could hear the excitement in their voices. Where other young men from the village had gone on quests to never return, Woo Jin would be victorious. Great was his destiny.

The pressure of their expectations pressed upon

him. Woo Jin recognized with sudden clarity that what his instructors had lectured about had now arrived. He had always thought it would come under the onslaught of an opponent's blade, but he was wrong. Woo Jin realized two choices stood before him: either he would fall in defeat under the stress of this moment, or he would stand tall and fight to win.

Woo Jin focused on his breathing. He pushed the whirlwind of conflicting thoughts out of his mind. As his dojang instructors had taught him, he concentrated only upon the now. The past and future no longer existed as he dealt with the present.

"I am ready," he said, startling himself with the steadiness of his voice. The concern in his mother's face fell away to fierce pride. Woo Jin turned and bowed to this father, then to the gathered villagers.

"I will return in several weeks," he announced. Mining for confidence, he found the emotion, and it bubbled up to his face as a wide, easy smile.

He spun on his heels and strode to the horse at the edge of their property. A hostler had placed his belongings on the steed's back, and now waited, holding the reins. Woo Jin was surprised the hostler wore a sword on his back. Strife between villages was uncommon on the island, though after the meeting this morning, he realized that perhaps conflict and violence were more common than he thought. Jeju held secrets that Woo Jin couldn't have even guessed existed before today.

"I ride to Jeju-si," Woo Jin informed the hostler as he checked to make sure everything he needed had been placed on the horse. He had three swords, two daggers, a quiver with two dozen of the village's finest arrows, and his favorite bow. The secreted away pyeon-jeons and bow that Official Yeo had given him were of far greater quality, however.

"Will someone be there to retrieve the horse?" he asked the hostler. "I won't be back for days, or perhaps weeks."

The hostler waved Woo Jin's concern aside. "I will be in Jeju-si when you arrive." He handed Woo Jin the reins.

"But you have no horse. You'll travel to Jeju-si on foot?"

The hostler nodded. "I'll run there. Let me know where you would like to drop off the horse, and I'll collect it there."

Woo Jin inspected the hostler closer. He wore a tan hanbok, the loose cloth settling over the curves of his muscle. Woo Jin had never seen anyone with such a defined physique. The hostler looked to be Woo Jin's age, his face young and clean shaven. Despite his impressive build, he couldn't be serious about reaching the city before someone on horseback.

"You will run to Jeju-si? It takes most of the day to ride there. On foot, it will take at least two days."

The hostler's smile brightened. "Please, don't worry. I'm fast, and I'm strong. The horse will be taken care of when you arrive. You need but tell me your destination."

Woo Jin patted the steed's flank, shaking his head. "This has been a strange morning," he muttered. "I wonder if the entire quest will be as full of surprises."

The hostler's eyes widened. "You're going on the quest tomorrow?"

Woo Jin hesitated, cautious at the hostler's sudden attention. "I am," he admitted, glancing again at the sword on the hostler's back. In the past, Woo Jin had looked at the people of Jeju as extended family. What his father said earlier had been true. Woo Jin seldom left the village, the martial arts dojang which he attended being the only exception. Visitors came to his village often, however, and they always seemed kind and honest. Now he wondered if this sword-wielding stranger from a different region of the island was friend or foe.

"Then we will converse more in the coming days," the hostler said. "Where will you be staying? I will retrieve the horse there."

Woo Jin hesitated. Meeting the sword-carrying hostler alone in the big city daunted him, but he had no choice. He had to reveal his resting place for the night, so said, "The Seacrest Inn. Do you know it?"

The hostler nodded. "I have passed it before. I promise to be there when you arrive, so I will start off now. Until we will meet again."

He turned to the road and started off at a walk that fell into a jog. His powerful legs pumped beneath him as the jog became a run, then a dash that kicked up dirt under the leather boots he wore. Before Woo Jin knew it, the hostler had disappeared around the bend.

Conscious of eyes on him, Woo Jin mounted the horse, waved to his parents and the villagers in final parting, then rode off. The narrow path he took joined the major road leading to Jeju-si. As he passed the oreum, he pulled the horse to a halt under the trees. Reaching into his pack, he retrieved one of his three swords and strapped it to his waist. He considered stringing the bow but decided against it. He didn't want to appear as if he was riding to war.

Woo Jin inhaled the leafy trees' and flowering plants' familiar smells. He had spoken bravely before, but his confidence slipped as the unknown loomed before him. He felt alone and at the beginning of a dark road whose end stretched too far to see. Would he ever return to his mother, father, and village?

He couldn't retreat now, not when so much rested on him going forward. Snapping the reins, he set the horse at a slow trot down the same path the hostler took to Jeju-si.

3

Woo Jin's hand drifted to the hilt of his sword at the rustling of leaves and the sudden snapping of twigs. The horse sensed his tension and broke into a skittish run several times when Woo Jin's legs contracted too tightly against its flanks. The winding lane they took eventually joined the wide road going north to Jeju-si.

After leaving the forests, Woo Jin saw other travelers heading in the same direction. Whereas before the company of islanders from different villagers would have been welcoming, now he attempted to keep a distance between himself and those around him.

The day drew on, the sun rising high in the sky to descend as evening approached. The tall gates of Jeju-si rose up in the distance. Woo Jin merged into a throng of merchants coming in from the surrounding villages to sell their wares in the busy night market by Jeju-si's harbors. Twenty-four hours a day, Jeju-si, so close to the mainland of South Hanguk, bustled with life.

Guards wielding tall halberds with thick wooden handles topped by wicked curved blades stood at the portico of the gate surrounding the city and inspected each visitor entering this time of evening.

Woo Jin breathed in and out evenly as he came under one of the guard's stern gaze.

"What's your business for visiting Jeju-si tonight?"

"I'm traveling to the Seacrest Inn," Woo Jin replied. He relaxed his posture and bowed his head to the guard. "I'm to stay there for the night to meet the governor tomorrow."

The guard's eyes widened. "You're questing?"

Woo Jin maintained an even breath. "Indeed I am."

The guard smiled. "Go with bravery and come back in honor!" The guard bowed to Woo Jin, then stepped aside to allow passage.

Woo Jin waved at the man as he passed through the portico, a weight lifting from his shoulders. He rode into the sprawling city. The buildings of black brick spread out along narrow lanes in an intricate maze around him. Many of the establishments that lined the main roads stood two stories high. Here and there, Woo Jin saw actual glass in the windows reflecting the pale light of the moon and stars. In the villages, they only had gauze paper panes to let in light, and these were covered by heavy wooden shutters keeping out the cold in the winter.

Merchants hawked their wares in booming voices. Their claims of the best quality at the cheapest prices competed for attention in the street. Customers sat outside of bustling restaurants and drank beer and soju, while waiters cooked meat over steaming grills. On the island, Jeju-si was the epicenter of fashion and culture. Women dressed in finely made hanboks dyed in bright spring colors of green, yellow, and blue, their faces done in heavy white makeup. Whenever he caught the eye of a passing girl, Woo Jin's heart raced and he quickly looked away.

Entranced by the sights and sounds around him, he became lost in the winding city streets. He paused to ask guards stationed along the roads for directions to Seacrest Inn. When they asked his business, he informed them he would meet the governor tomorrow for a quest. Each guard reacted the same as the first. With encouraging words and bright smiles, they pointed out the lane Woo Jin should take, and wished him great success on his undertaking.

Their responses were more like what Woo Jin had expected as a questing male, which was why the early morning meeting with the government official had surprised him. Only the bravest young men requested quests to prove their prowess to their peers. Of those that journeyed, only the best came back alive to claim praise from the governor, and eventually glory from the Emperor of South Hanguk.

At last, Woo Jin reached the inn where his father had reserved a room for him. As promised, the hostler waited nearby. To Woo Jin's relief, he saw the hostler still had the sword hung on his back, which made an easy unsheathing of it impossible. The hostler bowed as

Woo Jin dismounted. He unpacked Woo Jin's belongings, handed them to him, then took the reins.

"He didn't give you any trouble, did he?" the hostler asked, patting the horse's nose.

Woo Jin shook his head. "He travelled well. He was great company, and we made good time." He studied the hostler. "You don't look tired. Did you really run all the way here?"

"I did," the hostler replied, "but I arrived a couple of hours ago and have rested some. I must bring the mare to the stable my uncle rents here in the city. Someone else will take her back to the farms tomorrow."

Woo Jin nodded. "Well, I should secure my room now. It was nice to make your acquaintance."

"Will you be having dinner soon?" the hostler asked as Woo Jin turned away to the inn.

Woo Jin paused. "I will."

"After I've returned the mare, I will be free. I'm not staying at this inn for the night, but my lodgings are just the other lane over. If you have time, please join me for dinner. We can speak of the quest tomorrow."

Woo Jin swallowed in a throat gone dry. He tried to remain casual as he looked the hostler over again. He saw no other weapons besides that sword, but perhaps the hostler had something hidden that he planned to use later. Had Official Yeo somehow learned that Woo Jin revealed the plan to assassinate the foreigner to his father? How could that be possible? He and his father had discussed the assignment high up on the oreum. With his own eyes, Woo Jin had seen the official walk away down the lane through the trees.

Had he circled back to spy on Woo Jin?

"I'm quite tired after my long trip here," Woo Jin said, "and should get to bed after dinner."

The hostler seemed reluctant to leave, but acquiesced. "Then I'll see you again tomorrow morning," he said as he led the horse away.

"Tomorrow morning?" The question came out harsher than Woo Jin intended. The hostler's stubbornness was confounding and wearing down his patience. "I will meet the governor early in order to begin my quest."

The hostler paused. "I know. And so will I. My name is Kang Ha Jun, and I am one of the companions who will join this quest with you."

4

Woo Jin watched the hostler leave, a whirlwind of thoughts circling in his mind. Had Official Yeo sent Ha Jun to spy on him? Did the official trust him so little? Did he think that Woo Jin could not, or would not, murder the foreigner when the opportunity arose?

Woo Jin dined at a popular seafood restaurant near the inn. Customers filled the tables around him, and waiters wove between them with platters of freshly caught fish that filled the air with the heavy aroma of the sea. Woo Jin had been seated alone on a mat on the floor, a spread of abalone before him. Side dishes of kimchi, oysters, shrimp, and crab encircled the fish.

His father had given him a little extra to spend so that he could splurge before he started the difficult journey tomorrow. Woo Jin had chosen Jeju's abalone, which was known around South Hanguk for its delicate taste and high price. Yet each time Woo Jin dipped the cool slices of fish in wasabi sauce and placed it in his mouth, he found it wouldn't slide down his throat. He chewed the flesh until it was mush in his mouth, but the only way he could choke it down was by taking large gulps of beer until his head swam.

After the meal, Woo Jin stumbled to his room, the walls spinning as he collapsed on the pallet. His lodging was small, the floors swept and clean. A Hallabang orange had been set out on the table should he get hungry during the night. The eternal Jeju breeze whistled through the inn. A basin of water had been set up for Woo Jin to bathe in when he rose in the morning. He gazed through the window at the velvet black sky full of stars, the moon a bright crescent above the island. He had set his pack in a corner against the wall but kept his dagger at the ready. Only a curtain separated his room from the others, and Woo Jin wouldn't be caught unaware and defenseless if attacked during the night.

He closed his eyes tight so that he could no longer see the rotating walls and tried to force sleep to come. He didn't want to stand in front of the governor tomorrow appearing haggard, and he didn't want to start the quest exhausted. He knew not what dangers he would face soon, but he realized that they were very real and could happen at any moment. Quests were unpredictable, the success rate very low. Only the bravest young men seeking the greatest fortune undertook them. The rewards, if successfully completed, were incredibly high.

No matter how much he tried, however, Woo Jin

couldn't shut off his mind. Several times, he managed to doze off, only to snap awake at a noise drifting up from the streets, or the sound of other lodgers seeping in from nearby rooms. For a short time late at night, the voices quieted outside of the inn. Even before light from the new day touched the sky, however, the rumble of wagons from fishermen coming back from the sea resounded through the streets. Woo Jin realized he wouldn't get any more sleep, so he stripped off his clothes and wiped himself down with water from the basin.

After dressing, he went to a nearby restaurant. Drunk fishermen crowded the tables, cups of soju surrounding their meals as their work day ended and they prepared to retire for the day. Boisterous laughter greeted Woo Jin as the waiter showed him to a table in the corner. Woo Jin ordered a light breakfast of fish porridge and drank a draught of expensive ginseng. The invigorating tonic had a sharp, bitter taste that assaulted his tongue and burned the back of his throat. Fatigue dropped from him with each swallow, his senses sharpening to a knife's edge, his heart pounding and his mood lifting as his strength returned.

His appetite awakened with a deep rumble in his stomach. Woo Jin finished his meal, leapt from the table to pay the bill, and returned to his room. He gathered his belongings and strapped his two swords to his hip. He slung the third sword over his shoulder and carried his new bow and quiver in their waterproof pack.

Unlike the inn, Woo Jin easily located the governor's office. The only three-story structure in Jeju-si, the tall office stood above all else in the city. It had no walls to symbolize transparency, and had a high steepled roof supported by thick pillars. A single chair, ornately carved, occupied the center of the wooden floor and faced the city. A spiked gate surrounded the office.

After stating his business to the guards stationed there, Woo Jin entered the official grounds. The governor had not yet arrived, but several of his retainers stood on the steps leading up to the platform and chair. For the first time in his sixteen years, Woo Jin saw the foreigner. He stared in wonder at her, mouth slightly agape as he struggled to comprehend the strangeness of her appearance.

So, this was who Official Yeo had commissioned him to kill?

If Woo Jin hadn't been told that the foreigner was female, he might not have realized her sex. Her skin was velvet like the night sky and seemed to absorb the sunlight. Her hair bore the same pale luminescence of the moon and cascaded down her back as a wild mane to her hips. She wore a cream-colored robe with high collar that extended above her pointed ears. Blue swirls ran down the robe in elaborate designs, and a black and blue belt was wrapped around her slender hips. Despite the warm spring weather, the foreigner wore fingerless fur lined gloves.

She stood alone at the foot of the stairs leading to the governor's chair. Seven young men stood across from her. One of them was the hostler, Ha Jun, a single sword on his hip and a firelance slung over his shoulder. Woo Jin didn't want to engage in conversation with Ha Jun, especially in front of the six young men who stood next to him. They must be the other companions of their questing group. Their number surprised Woo Jin as he had been taught that groups of four went on quests. This was not only tradition, but it also ensured that the heroic deeds of each young man could stand out among the others.

Woo Jin wanted to introduce himself to the other six companions who he would soon call brothers, but hesitated. He felt awkward standing alone but couldn't bring himself to stand near the last person of the group, the solitary Dark Elf. Everything about her was hideous. How could a person have such dark skin, and hair that pale color? He found it difficult to tear his eyes away from the strangeness of her appearance. Beneath her clothes, he wondered if she was female in the same manner that the woman of South Hanguk were female? Perhaps mysterious organs he couldn't even imagine lurked beneath her robes.

The shrill blowing of trumpets announcing the arrival of the governor jerked Woo Jin from his thoughts. A procession of aides walked down the lane towards the governor's office. Within their midst, four retainers in round hats, white billowing pants, and black gowns, carried the golden gama of the governor. They walked with practiced grace, the gama swaying with each step. When they reached the gate, the retainers set the gama down. The governor pulled back the silk curtain and stepped out. Woo Jin, along with everyone else in attendance, bowed low. As the governor walked by to ascend the steps of his official office, Woo Jin noticed out of the corner of his eye that the foreigner remained erect, not lowering her head like the rest of them.

Sudden anger spiked through him, but since no one else commented, Woo Jin remained silent.

The governor took his seat in the chair facing the city. The waiting attendants moved forward and gathered on either side of him, scrolls in their hands. The hostler and the six other companions climbed the stairs and went to bended knee before the governor. Woo Jin couldn't put it off any longer. He joined them, taking the position in the line of young men opposite the hostler. The foreigner also ascended the platform but stood facing the companions.

The governor opened his arms and said in a booming voice, "Welcome, young warriors of Jeju Island! It is with great pride that I send you out upon the mainland to make a name for yourselves amongst your peers. I have studied the current affairs of our great country, and I have decided upon a quest that will truly elevate your status should you come back victorious."

He reached out to an official, who handed him a scroll. The governor unrolled it and read the contents, a grave expression carving its way into his face.

"The preparations have been met. This, indeed, is a most important quest that you will undertake. Our country of South Hanguk, which has been at war with North Hanguk for generations, has left many cities on the ever-shifting borders in ruins. In one such place, there is said to be Goseong, a village of children and women. A fresh eruption in conflict has sent their men off fighting to protect their lands from the ravaging armies of the Child-God of North Hanguk. The Emperor of South Hanguk would like all of these border villages evacuated but cannot spare the soldiers at this precarious time as they hold off the Child-God's most potent threat: dragons.

"And so, this quest has been issued to the provinces of South Hanguk with the hope that heroes will ride out and save the children and women from the onslaught of the Child-God of the North."

The governor gazed down at the eight companions on bended knee before him. "On this most important of missions, many young men from other provinces will not return. Rarely have I seen a quest as difficult as this, and that is why the usual number of four in a questing group has become eight. You young men from the island of Jeju, who have mastered the arts of war, will succeed where others would fail. Today, you set forth from Jeju as nameless warriors. When you return, you will be that much closer to being named heroes!"

5

The warning that dragons might swoop down upon the village of Goseong stopped Woo Jin's heart. If the winged beasts became aware of the companions' presence as they evacuated the children and women from the border village, what could they do? How would they prevail?

Woo Jin glanced at the seven young men on bended knee beside him. Their faces had paled, and he realized that they were thinking the same thing. Death on leathery wings. Acid, fire, and ice, the fearsome dragons' breath. Screams as flesh burned from bones, lungs broiled in chests, and limbs melted away to stain the moist earth. The people of South Hanguk had all heard rumors of the destructive capabilities of dragons. Now Woo Jin and his companions would step into the monsters' domain to cower at the edges of the nightmare that resided there.

"You must enter the village of children in secret,"

the governor said. "It is imperative that you do not draw the dragons' attention, but it is believed this will not be an issue. Our Emperor has sent a large contingent of soldiers to secure the northern peaks of Seollaksan Mountains. In response, the Child-God has ordered his dragons to burn down any fortifications they find. For you eight, all you should face as you rescue the villagers are North Hanguk troops patrolling the border. They will be no match for you."

The governor rolled up the scroll and handed it back to the official. "I have absolute confidence in the success of your mission. Especially you," he said, his gaze fastened on Woo Jin. "Boasts of your skills in martial combat are regularly repeated throughout the island. You are destined to be triumphant. You are fated to become a hero!"

Woo Jin's seven companions turned to him, eyes opened wide in astonishment at the governor's praise. A flurry of emotions raged through Woo Jin at the sudden attention focused upon him, but he pushed the nervousness down and bowed to the governor.

"I will do all that I can to not disappoint the people of Jeju," Woo Jin said in a humble voice.

The governor nodded. "Now, go with the official. He will inform you of the remaining details of your journey. When you return to the island in good health and in success, we will meet again in celebration."

The eight companions stood and followed the official carrying the scroll back down the steps to the gate. Like a shadow of dark tidings, the foreigner hovered behind them.

The official turned to the companions. "A ferry has been arranged to take you across the Hanguk Strait to the city of Busan. From there, you'll travel by horse to the border of North Hanguk. There's no timetable for you to arrive, but do not delay. We believe that other provinces may send groups of their own companions on the same quest, as it has become well known amongst the governors that the Emperor would like to have the border towns evacuated. The one you travel to now, Goseong, is of highest priority because of the age of its occupants."

The official reached into his hanbok and removed a money pouch. He turned to the companion who rested a two-handed sword, the blade as tall as a person, in a sheath against his shoulder. "You, Kim In-Su, are the eldest of the group. It will be you who lead your younger brothers on this journey."

The official handed the pouch to In-Su, who placed the coins in the folds of his red hanbok.

"You will be in charge of the allotted funds. This should be more than enough to get you to the border, but you'll have nothing to waste, and there'll be many times when your bellies will rumble with hunger. Stay in inns only when you cannot sleep outside, and be frugal in your meals."

The official bowed to the eight gathered men. "Now go quickly and return on swift feet. The people of Jeju await the tales of your heroism."

Woo Jin and his companions bowed low to the official as he took his leave. Then the seven younger brothers bowed to In-Su, who returned the gesture.

"I am honored to travel with you on this quest to Goseong," In-Su said. He then asked the other seven companions their names and ages. Woo Jin discovered that he was the youngest, and to his dismay, the same age as Ha Jun.

Once they completed their introductions, In-Su said, "We'll have time to talk later. The docks aren't far from here, and we have a ferry to catch. You all have provisions to last you for a couple of days?"

The seven brothers said they did. They turned towards the dock, but Ha Jun spoke up.

"I apologize, elder brother," he said with a bow to In-Su. "I believe there is someone else who may like to speak."

In-Su looked at Ha Jun, puzzled. "Everyone present has been accounted for," he replied. Realization slowly dawned on his face. A frown turned his lips, and he glanced at the foreigner standing near them. He looked back at Ha Jun.

"I'm sure she has nothing to say to us," he said. "Her purpose is to record our adventure. She's not to take part in it or interfere with our affairs in any way."

Without waiting for Ha Jun to respond, In-Su started towards the docks. The rest followed, and Woo Jin joined them. He knew he shouldn't, but he couldn't help but look over his shoulder to see if Ha Jun was close behind. Since they were the same age, they would have to be friends on the journey. Ha Jun, however, had hesitated. Woo Jin overheard him say something to the foreigner and stumbled in surprise that the hostler *wasn't* speaking in Korean.

34

The revelation created eddies in Woo Jin's mind that made him dizzy. Ha Jun spoke to the foreigner in an alien language. Was it Windshine's native language? Who had taught Ha Jun the elvish tongue? What was his relationship to the female elf who Woo Jin had been commissioned to kill?

Woo Jin's gut feeling about Ha Jun may have been right all along. The hostler could not be trusted.

6

Woo Jin kept close to his older brothers, not wanting to be left in the company of Ha Jun. The hostler lagged several steps behind him. The foreigner remained at the periphery of the companions as they made their way to the docks. To Woo Jin's relief, she made no attempt to come closer to them. Since she had accompanied young men on quests before, she probably knew where they were going better than the companions did.

Woo Jin noticed In-Su glance back at Ha Jun, then to his left at the foreigner. Worry creased his elder brother's brow. Woo Jin wished to ask him what he knew about the hostler, but even in the early morning, Jeju bustled with people heading back and forth to the port. The islanders shipped their wares to the mainland, which sold at expensive prices since Jeju people made the traditional goods by hand.

The sharp cries of seagulls circling in the sky

greeted them as they reached the docks. Fishing boats filled the harbor, bobbing up and down in the undulating waves. Small restaurants, some with only three or four tables, ran along the docks, their tables filled with customers eating seafood caught fresh during the night. Crab, squid, eel, and a wide array of fish still wriggled on plates as diners flayed them and ate the glistening meat off their spindly bones.

Jeju boasted several ferry companies. The governor had reserved a service for the companions, and they walked up the bobbing gangplank to be met by a swarthy man with a wide brimmed black hat, puffy white shirt and black pants. He eyed Ha Jun as he inhaled from a long pipe settled at the edge of his lips. Ha Jun didn't make eye contact, and instead gazed out at the white waves of the Strait.

The sailor cast a hard stare at the foreigner hanging back from the rest of the group. In a gruff but resigned voice, he said, "Well, come aboard, then."

The ferry's crew bore the same open hostility to the foreigner's presence. Woo Jin inched his hand to the hilt of his blade, but when he thought about it, he didn't know where the danger lay. The Dark Elf was not his ally. How much would that matter, though, since the foreigner was currently a part of their questing group? If the deckhands attacked her while on the Hanguk Strait, he could get swept up in the melee. He may not be on her side, and he would eventually have to kill her; but his mission was a secret that no one else could discover or his family would be in danger. If someone attacked her, he would have to defend the foreigner so as not to arouse suspicion.

These crewmen must know something nefarious about the foreigner to gaze at her in such a manner. But as one of the swarthy men led the companions into the cargo hold, Woo Jin wondered why they regarded Ha Jun with the same level of animosity.

Crates of various sizes were stacked against the sides of the hull. Like the cargo ships, the ferries carried goods, but they also had room for passengers, who they trans-ported twice daily. The companions sat upon the sturdier crates, settling in for the daylong journey to Busan. Because of the size of the cargo hold, they couldn't put much distance between themselves and the Dark Elf. Woo Jin forced himself not to stare at her, though he picked up a stinging sweet scent from her. Again, he wondered what her naked body looked like beneath her exotic clothes.

A sudden jerk of the boat told them they had cast off. Overhead, they heard the first mate shouting commands and the patter of feet rushing across the deck as the crewmen followed his orders.

"Will we ever see our homes again?" one of the companions, who had introduced himself as Jae Jin, murmured. The shortest of the group, he had a wide, portly girth. Twin swords with flat, curved blades hung on his hips, and he wore brown leather armor over the top of his red hanbok and white pants.

Woo Jin met his eyes in solemn contemplation, but it was In-Su who answered.

"Very few men come back from these quests. It is

why most never undertake the journey in the first place. These tests of heroism are voluntary. They give men the opportunity to distinguish themselves in a way that being a soldier cannot."

He looked from one of them to the other. "Of the eight of us, who here has done their mandatory service in the Emperor's army?"

Only one, Lim Kun Woo, raised his hand.

"It's been several years since I did my mandatory service," In-Su continued. "It's an honor to serve one's country, but ultimately, in your units, you are one of a whole. We fought scrimmages, but we have been in a stalemate with North Hanguk for generations. A full fledge conflict hasn't happened since our father's father's time, and there's little chance to prove your worth when you spend most of your enlistment watching the other side waiting for them to make a move."

"What are they like?" Jae Jin asked. "The people of North Hanguk?"

In-Su sighed. "If you push far into the country, you'll find they're hungry. The Child-God puts all their resources into maintaining his army, and not into farming and tending the land. It is said that South Hanguk has three times the population of North Hanguk, yet we still cannot get the upper hand. The Child-God's magic is great, and the soldiers of North Hanguk, though fewer, are formidable in combat. All the efforts of their people have only one purpose: war. It has become intertwined in their very spirits."

In-Su lowered his voice. "In the Emperor's forces,

it's whispered, but never spoken in the vicinity of generals, that a solider of North Hanguk is worth three of South Hanguk's soldiers."

"And soon we will be facing them," Jae Jin said.

Woo Jin clapped Jae Jin on the back. "Our eldest brother will devise a plan to defeat our enemies so we can evacuate the village of Goseong. Don't worry!"

In-Su smiled. "That is true. We have many good men here. I will need to see how each one handles himself as we travel to Goseong before I can devise a strategy. But our youngest brother is right. We will be victorious."

He turned to Woo Jin. "Your skill with the sword, dagger, and arrow is well-known on the island. We will need everything you can give if we are to succeed."

Woo Jin bowed even as his thoughts raced. He would have to carefully listen to the plans In-Su crafted as they approached the village of children. He would also have to study the Dark Elf to glean what her fighting abilities were, if they existed at all. She was female, which meant that she would be the weakest of them. But the foreigners may have strange powers, and he couldn't let his guard down. When the time was right, maybe in the heat of battle, the opportunity to slay her would present itself. In the meantime, he couldn't let his brothers see the pyeonjeons or discover the poison he had stored away in his bag.

At this point, Woo Jin couldn't even guess how he would get away with this, but he must. For his family's sake, the foreigner must die on this quest if he was to ever return to Jeju.

7

The narrow confines of the cargo hold made private conversation impossible. As the boat cut through waves that echoed against the hull, the eight companions introduced themselves and their family backgrounds. Woo Jin learned that Ha Jun belonged to one of the most prosperous farming families on the island. They produced Hallabangs, the fist-sized oranges that were distinctive to Jeju. The rich volcanic soil gave the oranges a full-bodied, sweet taste that suffused the mouth as fragranced juice leaked down the chin from fleshly slices. Off the island, only the wealthy could afford them. The oranges were considered a rare delicacy that Ha Jun said was also transported to foreign countries.

Three of the companions, Jang Jae Jin, Jang Ki Ha, and Jang Jae Ho, were brothers and came from musical backgrounds. Several instruments hung from their shoulders or on straps around their necks, the largest of which was a drum carried on the back of the most muscular of their trio.

"To have three *champions of the spirit* journey with us is indeed fortunate," In-Su said. "When I served, we rarely even had one in each battalion. Only on the most important missions did a musician join us. Their arts are highly prized by the generals in the heat of battle."

The oldest of the three brothers, the drum carrier, Ki Ha, nodded. "We will serve the Emperor after this quest. Our family has developed a new melody, more potent than any that has ever been performed before. But it must be tested in conflict before we bring it before the Emperor and place our talents in His service. Once He discovers what we have developed, our family's name will become known throughout South Hanguk and beyond."

The final member of the company was a monk, Geun Nam-Kyu. He wore gray robes, and a golden pendant of a three-legged crow hung around his neck. Hanging from his belt were more than a dozen short daggers with hoops attached to their hilts. The weapons went completely around his waist and clanked against each other with a metallic jingle when he moved.

Unlike the rest of them, Nam-Kyu stared at the Dark Elf. He had waited until she sat down so that he could position himself in her line of sight, and his eyes didn't stray from her black face. Woo Jin knew she must feel Nam-Kyu's gaze upon her, but she made no outward sign of acknowledgement, and didn't return his stare.

In-Su seemed embarrassed to have to bring the

group's attention to the situation between the staring monk and the silent foreigner. He said, "As the second eldest, I will need your wisdom and advice above all others, brother."

Nam-Kyu blinked and turned away from the Dark Elf. "Any helpful words I can offer you, I will without hesitation."

A look passed between them that Woo Jin couldn't decipher. He needed to find a moment to speak to his companions, but it was only after they docked in Busan and stepped out of the boat into a day that had turned to night that he found his chance.

The buildings of Busan, one of South Hanguk's largest cities, sprouted up from the ground in bunches and stood so close to each other that there was almost no space between them. Night markets kept the docks busy, the number of people walking the twisting lanes dwarfing that of Jeju.

The companions had to squeeze their way through the bustling crowds. Unlike on the island, numerous foreigners conducted trade in the ports of Busan. From dark olive to tan to swarthy skin, people from nearby countries imported and exported rare goods from around the world. Guards wearing tall red hats wandered the ports to ensure that the foreigners didn't leave the area for the interior of South Hanguk, which was forbidden and punishable by death through slow torture.

Despite the greater diversity of people, everyone was human. Windshine was the only non-human, and the only one with such dark skin. Heads turned to regard her as she passed through the port. Like before, she gave the companions a wide berth, and Woo Jin worried about losing her in the pulsating throng of people.

He wasn't alone in that concern, as In-Su muttered, "She should stay closer to us. But she draws so much attention that it's more comfortable if she keeps a distance."

"She's aware of that," Nam-Kyu said, his voice low. "Never underestimate her. She has accompanied men on these quests many times going back generations. She knows what she's doing."

Woo Jin glanced over his shoulder to see how close Ha Jun followed them. Once again, he trailed several steps behind. In-Su waved him to catch up with them and said, "You're familiar with steeds, and we're in need of nine to get on our way to Goseong. Ask around and see where we can get the best price for the fastest, strongest horses."

"We won't stay the night in Busan?" Ha Jun asked.

In-Su shook his head.

"We may not be the only group on this quest. Since we come from the island, we have farther to go than any traveling straight from a province here on the mainland."

Ha Jun assured them he would not be gone long, then stepped into a different stream of people and allowed himself to be carried along by the momentum of those around him. In-Su led the remaining seven to a food stall where they ordered fresh squid, which the attendant placed on a coal fire and baked right in front of them. In-Su scanned the area as they tore the squid into strips and passed it among themselves. The elf had once again taken up a position some distance from them. She stood in the shadows of a nearby building, almost disappearing into the inky pools except for her pale hair that stood out in stark contrast to the darkness engulfing her.

"The journey to Goseong should be uneventful," In-Su said to the group. "As we near the border between South and North Hanguk, we'll have to proceed more carefully. There's more than one reason that we must evacuate the village of children. North Hanguk soldiers kidnap young girls to bring back to their country and force them to bear children. The Child-God is said to have developed a potion that ensures the women of North Hanguk bear boys instead of girls, but this has left them with a deficiency of females to mate with."

"Why don't the border villages evacuate those regions?" Jae Jin asked.

Here, the monk answered. "They have been living in those lands for generations, and their ancestors are buried there. The villagers are reluctant to abandon their forbears. They consider it sacrilege to do so."

In-Su nodded. "This is why the Emperor has allowed the border villagers to remain, despite the danger they're always in. But the Child-God has taken to systematically evading them, killing the men, and abducting the girls and women. The Elder of Goseong sent a message to the Emperor imploring for aid while the men held back the North Hanguk soldiers for as long as they could. It is a small village with only eight or nine dozen inhabitants. A few veterans should have remained behind as a last resort to defend against abductors. They will aid us in moving the children and women from Goseong to the closest South Hanguk city."

He looked around at the seven companions gathered close around him. "We're only a small group, but each of us are the best of our peers. It's why we were chosen to go on this quest." In-Su focused on Woo Jin. "We have the highest expectations from you, little brother."

Woo Jin nodded. "I will give all I have and more to aid you in any way I can."

"The only difficulty on the journey to Goseong," In-Su said, his voice almost inaudible to a point that the six companions had to lean in close to hear him over the bustle of the port, "may be Kang Ha Jun. There are strange rumors surrounding him. It's hard to tell fact from fiction, but what I know for certain is that this isn't his first quest. This isn't the first time he has travelled in the company of the foreigner."

Woo Jin had surmised the latter when Ha Jun had spoken to the Dark Elf in her native tongue, but to think that the hostler, only as old as he, had already gone on a quest and come back alive was almost impossible to believe.

"When did he last travel in the company of the foreigner?" Jae Jin asked.

"Less than twelve months ago," In-Su replied. "I know the family of the solider that was one of his companions. Only that good man, Ha Jun and the Dark Elf returned to Jeju alive."

"I can verify this," Nam-Kyu added. "A monk of our order also travelled with them and didn't make it back from the quest. The last of their four-man group was the son of Seogwipo-si's mayor. They had set out for Naganeupseong Fortress to eradicate a demon that had taken root there. What they found, we may never know. But the monk and the politician's son paid for the journey with their lives."

"Death is the risk we take to ascend to legends," In-Su said. "Facing it down and prevailing is the price we pay to become heroes. Only the most courageous go on these journeys, and only the best return. Normally, when men come back from the trials they suffered, they boast of their deeds, and their countrymen gather around to hear with amazement. Songs are made of their heroic bouts, that then go on to inspire the hearts of their compatriots. This is tradition."

In-Su shook his head. "But when the soldier, Song Seong Min, returned from his quest with Ha Jun, he refused to speak about what happened. The people of his village gathered around his home and waited for him to emerge, but days passed in which he stayed inside with his wife and newborn son. Word of his behavior spread to nearby villagers, for Seong Min had been known for being a generous, open man, always willing to help others when the need arose. Talkative, he had many close friends, and visited with his neighbors often. All of that changed after the quest, and no one knows why he closed himself off from those he once called brothers."

"And now Ha Jun is a part of our group," Jae Jin

49

said with a heavy sigh. "His presence doesn't bode well for our eventual success."

Concern swept In-Su's face. "You're probably right. It's ill fate he was assigned to this quest alongside of us. But he's only one of our problems."

In-Su inclined his head in the direction of the Dark Elf. She still stood away from them in the shadows of the building that seemed to wrap around her in intimate embrace.

"The foreigner is protected by the governor," In-Su said, "but the people of the island have never trusted her, whom age does not touch. She is unnatural. Darkness follows her and brushes against all she meets."

Woo Jin dared not lift his eyes in her direction. Doubt and chaos swirled his thoughts like a typhoon, and at the center of the maelstrom was his mission: to assassinate the Dark Elf, Windshine.

8

The seven companions fell silent and chewed on strips of squid at Ha Jun's approach through the night crowd.

"There is a nearby stable that rents horses at a fair price," he said. "But we'll have to put down a deposit."

"We'll be traveling a long way with them so that's reasonable. Lead the way," In-Su said.

They followed Ha Jun through the port's twisting lanes until they reached a long, wooden building with two-dozen stalls. The stable master met them at the gate and led them onto the grounds of thick, knotted grass. The smell of fresh dung and the neighing of horses, awoken at this late hour, greeted them.

"They'll ride far, and they'll ride fast," the stable master said, and directed the grooms carrying lanterns to bring eight horses from the stable stalls. The steeds all had dark brown coats except for one, which had mottled brown and white hair.

"They're battled tested, and it seems your group's riding into trouble." The stable master gave their swords and daggers a meaningful look. "I raised these horses by hand from when they were only foals. I've trained them to match the courage of their riders, so I'm selective who I rent them out to. If you be brave men, they'll ride into conflict without hesitation. Work together and be true to each other, and you and the steeds'll come back alive."

The stable master peered at the Dark Elf standing within the yard but at a distance from them. The flickering light from the torches created menacing shadows around her that seemed to writhe with sinister life.

"We meet again." The stable master bowed.

Woo Jin caught his breath that the man actually spoke to her. He couldn't help but cast a quick glance of suspicion at Ha Jun. Perhaps it hadn't been a good idea to have him go alone to find the mounts that would take them to Goseong. The stable master, in simple tan robes and a domed black hat with a tassel, seemed honest enough, but one never knew what mischief lurked in a man's heart. Perhaps Ha Jun, the Dark Elf, and this horse stable master had previous dealings, and had already concocted some tragedy to befall the companions once they were on the road from Busan.

The stable master didn't ease Woo Jin's suspicions when he said to Windshine, "I know *you'll* be coming back. Once more, my best steed's yours to ride."

An uncomfortable silence fell upon the companions. Woo Jin and his older brothers shifted uneasily from foot to foot at the stable master's pronouncement. Ha

Jun, Woo Jin noticed, had no such disquieted response, and simply stood, relaxed, as if the implications of the stable master's comment didn't include him as well.

"I'll need to know how long you'll be gone." The stable master looked at In-Su again. "Where're you headed?"

"A border village," In-Su responded. "Goseong."

"That'll be a week there and a week back, at least. How long you'll linger there?"

"It should only be a handful of days." In-Su rubbed his beard in thought. "We'll have to work out some things with the village elders, but we'll be moving fast so as not to acquire too much attention from the Child-God's soldiers. I would guess we'll be in Goseong for fewer than three days."

"Then pay me a full month," the stable master said, "and I'll refund any additional days, and the deposit, when you return."

In-Su agreed to the man's terms and paid him the fee. The companions loaded the horses with their gear and mounted. The stable master advised them which lanes to follow along the outskirts of Busan that would take them quickly out of the gated city. They thanked him, and after he wished them a safe journey one last time, they trotted off the stable grounds towards the city gates.

A slip of a crescent moon cut through the sky full of stars. The night had gotten late, and Woo Jin hoped they would rest soon. Fatigue draped over him. His restlessness at the inn the night before, and the day trip by ferry, left him exhausted now. He struggled to keep his eyes open as they rode through the gates onto the road heading north. He forced his shoulders to stay straight, refusing to slump in front of his elder brothers and have them believe he would slow them down.

They rode in silence. When Woo Jin felt he couldn't stay on his saddle another moment, when he was digging his nails into his palms so he wouldn't slip into dreams bubbling up from his subconscious to drown his conscious, In-Su called for a halt.

"We'll keep watch in groups of two." In-Su handed two of the blood brothers, Ki Ha and Jae Ho, a long red candle with notches down its length. "Wake Ha Jun and Woo Jin when the candle has burned off four marks. They will take the second watch, and Jae Jin and Nam Kyu will take the third. Kun Woo and I will take the last and longest watch. We've served and are used to traveling far distances on little sleep."

Woo Jin appreciated the thought of having a long rest before resuming the journey the following morning, but he didn't like the idea of being paired with Ha Jun. In-Su would put them together like this often since the two of them shared the same age.

They tied the horses where there was plenty of grass for them to eat, then settled off the road under the trees. Woo Jin felt that as soon as he closed his eyes, a firm hand shook him awake. He blinked and looked around confused. Ki Ha stood over him, the candle burned down by four marks. It seemed like it had happened instantly.

Sleep didn't relinquish Woo Jin easily, figments of half-forgotten dreams hovering at the edges of his vision as he shook his head to clear it. Vertigo swept over him when he stood so that he stumbled.

"Sorry to wake you so soon, brother," Ki Ha said, his voice heavy with fatigue. "Time passes swiftly when you're sleep."

Woo Jin only nodded, the ability to form words lost in his exhaustion. He trudged to his sentry position and wrapped his arms around himself to stave off the night chill that gripped the forest. Ki Ha had already fallen asleep before Woo Jin realized that he should have waved off his elder brother's apology. It wasn't polite to leave Ki Ha feeling bad for having woken him. Woo Jin promised himself to be more considerate to his companions as the journey progressed.

Ha Jun had also been woken. He seemed alert and sat on an overturned tree. Woo Jin didn't want to engage in conversation with him and sat down on an uncomfortable moss-covered rock several paces away from the hostler. He struggled to stay awake, but the grogginess in his head increased. The phantoms, still lingering from the dreams of his brief sleep, closed in upon him, and Woo Jin found himself swaying as he struggled to remain upright. He avoided looking in Ha Jun's direction, not wanting to know if the hostler observed his desperate struggle to stay on guard.

"May I ask you a favor?" Ha Jun's voice broke the silence.

Woo Jin jerked upright, their gazes locked, and a moment passed before Woo Jin nodded. Ha Jun stood and came to stand next to him. Despite himself, Woo Jin almost sighed with relief at the prospect of conversation, hoping it would drive sleep from him, or at least keep it at bay.

"I have heard of your mastery at wielding the bow and arrow." Ha Jun sat on the rock beside him. "It has always been my weakest weapon. When there's time during the journey, I would greatly appreciate if you gave me a lesson. I promise I'll be a diligent and attentive student to any advice you impart upon me."

The mention of the tools Woo Jin would use to kill the Dark Elf was like a draught of cold water doused over him. Adrenaline coursed through him, his senses sharpening as if danger lurked nearby. Woo Jin scanned the area for the foreigner but didn't see her. In all this darkness, and with her velvet black skin, Woo Jin wasn't surprised. He realized that he would have to find a moment during the daylight hours to complete his mission, as he would be at a disadvantage if he tried to kill her at night. Such a strategy held its own risks, as a day kill would be harder to hide, and his companions must not discover he was the culprit.

How did Official Yeo expect Woo Jin to accomplish the assassination? The task seemed impossible under the current circumstances, yet if Woo Jin was to keep his family safe, he had no choice but to keep his eyes open for the perfect opportunity to strike.

"When there is time," he said to Ha Jun, though he barely paid attention to the hostler as he continued to scan the road and surrounding forest for the missing foreigner.

When Ha Jun didn't immediately respond, Woo Jin looked at him to discover that the hostler, too, was now staring out into the darkness, his hand on the hilt of his two-handed sword.

"Is something out there?" Ha Jun asked. "You seem to be searching for something. Have you sensed movement?"

Woo Jin thought fast. "I just wanted to make sure everyone was accounted for so there'd be no mistakes." He paused a beat before adding, "Where's the foreigner?"

"Oh." Ha Jun relaxed. "Windshine is just there."

He pointed into the darkness. Woo Jin peered in the direction Ha Jun indicated, and his heartbeat raced again. Several paces from where their elder brothers slept, he saw the foreigner. Unlike the men, she wasn't sleeping. She stood in the well of shadows of a tree, invisible unless one knew where to look. She must have covered her pale white hair, for not even that was visible.

"She doesn't like us much," Woo Jin commented.

"Why do you say that?"

Woo Jin turned back to Ha Jun. "She always keeps a distance. She hasn't tried speaking to us since we began the journey."

Ha Jun shrugged. "She's been on many of these quests. Generations of them. Windshine is meant to observe, not to interfere."

Ha Jun didn't hesitate to speak up for the foreigner, which surprised Woo Jin. He figured that if the two of them were plotting something against the group, he would be more tight-lipped, not wanting to appear in league with her. Woo Jin decided to press him for more information and perhaps glean a weakness of the foreigner to improve his chances of killing her.

"I've heard that you travelled with her? Before, on a quest?"

Ha Jun nodded. "It's been a little more than six months."

"So, it's true?" Woo Jin exclaimed in a hushed voice. "What was it like?"

Ha Jun inhaled and exhaled slowly. Sudden wrinkles spread out from his eyes as his mood darkened, and in the candlelight, he appeared older. "Death follows men on these journeys." His voice deepened, becoming solemn. "These quests are trials only few are meant to survive. The lucky few, I think."

Grief weighed down the features of Ha Jun's face, and he seemed to age far beyond his sixteen years. Woo Jin was reluctant to ask more questions, not wanting to bring back whatever memories plagued Ha Jun, but his curiosity got the better of him.

"But you came back."

"I came back." Ha Jun sighed. "That's how I know it's mostly luck. What we faced on our quest was powerful beyond imagination. It was the evil of men taken form. It was retribution. It was hatred. And ultimately, it was death, there in front of us, shoving us into our graves."

Woo Jin had stopped breathing, and could only stare, transfixed.

"To make it back from the village of children, for all of us to make it back," Ha Jun said, "we must stick together as a group. As brothers, we must fight as one. If we do that, we might win."

Woo Jin blinked. He wasn't part of the group. Not fully. He had his own mission, and his family's fate hung in the balance. What he had to do, and what his brothers had to do, did not fully align. After listening to Ha Jun, he wondered if his actions would be the thing that got them all killed?

9

As the companions rode to Goseong, Woo Jin studied the foreigner for weaknesses. To his eye, she appeared to be an easy mark. She carried no sword or dagger. She didn't pay much attention to her surroundings, and usually gazed ahead of her at the road they took as if nothing else was important except reaching their destination.

And then, of course, she wouldn't be a challenge because she was just a woman. Woo Jin had yet to meet a capable female fighter, though he'd seen women wield weapons before. But they didn't engage in the constant, harsh training as men did, and their prowess in combat reflected their lack of experience.

Even as Woo Jin thought this, however, a question niggled at the back of his mind. If the Dark Elf had accompanied men on these quests for generations, and if most of the men died as they faced overwhelming forces, then how had she survived? How had she managed to come back to Jeju alive, every single time?

Windshine may seem like an easy kill, but Woo Jin calculated he needed to assassinate her with extreme caution. He didn't know what abilities the foreigners had, but he knew he couldn't fail in his assignment.

They rode from the coast of South Hanguk into the mainland of the country. The mild temperature near the sea was lost, and the humidity increased. Flowers budding along the road spread their petals for the spring and filled the air with pollen. The companions were either sneezing or suffering from congested noses, their eyes watering and red. Wasps with large stingers buzzed by their heads. Mosquitoes droned in their ears as they tried to sleep at night and left behind bright red bites along their skin in the morning. Brown squirrels played in the green leaves of trees, and swift-footed rabbits darted through the underbrush of the forest floor. The sharp cries of birds emanated from above as they flitted through the canopy. In the evening, the drone of crickets created a monotonous symphony that drowned out all other noises as the sun sank into the horizon.

Between the gated cities and villages, bandits roamed. The group of companions was big, however, and heavily armed, so that they rode north to the border without an attempted robbery. What concerned In-Su more were strange creatures that lurked in the country-side. He had heard the rumors of tigers wandering desolate fields and forests in the guise of humans. These beasts attacked unwary travelers and took not only their possessions, but also their forms. Every night they kept watch, and as the week passed, Woo Jin became better at staying alert during his shift.

In-Su pushed them past inhabited villages, not wanting to waste a moment to potential competition from other provinces that may be traveling to Goseong. They passed large and small farms off the path and behind short stone walls. The vegetables were kept in neat rows, and scarecrows in wispy rags dotted the fields to scare large black crows that circled in the sky. They would occasionally see a flock of ravens wheeling in the air above the forests, and knew that somewhere nearby in the wild, death had found someone.

As promised, on the third day of their seven-day journey to the border, Woo Jin gave Ha Jun an archery lesson. He instructed Ha Jun to shoot at marks he placed on soft wood targets in the forest with the monk's chalk. Ha Jun's habit of pulling the string back and holding on as he narrowed in on the target took too long for any reasonable battle. Yet when Woo Jin pressured him to release the arrow faster, Ha Jun missed the target in his haste.

"You must remain calm," Woo Jin advised him. "Slow your breathing. Set your sight quickly and release with confidence. With a bow, you're attacking at a distance, so you have time. But your target is moving, evading, so you must act fast. Also, you're vulnerable to attack because you're focused on the far, not the immediate vicinity. You must do everything instantly, yet accurately. Watch."

In the distance, squirrels played in the trees ahead

of them. Ha Jun took the bow from Woo Jin, nocked an arrow and released it in one movement. It sped fast and true, striking a squirrel through the skull as it leapt from one branch to another and spearing it to the tree.

"Always aim for the kill," Woo Jin said, nocking another arrow and releasing it to pierce a second squirrel in the throat. "With a sword, you can swing until your arms are tired. With the bow, you only have so many arrows, and each one must count."

Woo Jin nocked a third arrow and released it. The shaft went through the final squirrel's forehead and lodged into the bark behind it, the dead animal swaying with the force of the blow.

Their elder brothers, watching as they finished their midday meal, applauded Woo Jin's excellent marksmanship. Nam-Kyu went to retrieve the squirrels, skinned them and soaked the thin strips of meat in a pouch of salt brine for later.

In-Su went to Woo Jin and said, "Little brother, your skill will be essential for our survival when we engage North Hanguk patrols. You and the three champions of the spirit must take the rear in battle while Ha Jun, Nam-Kyu, Kun Woo and I take the lead. It's imperative that you take out as many of the enemy as quickly as possible. How many arrows do you carry in your quiver?"

"Two dozen," Woo Jin replied. He didn't mention the pyeonjeons or the poison that the government official had given him to kill Windshine.

"Try to make each arrow count for a kill," In-Su said, "as we must be prepared to be outnumbered. But if we work together, we stand the best chance to prevail."

When they mounted their horses and started off again on the road heading north, Ha Jun fell in beside Woo Jin. "Thank you, friend," Ha Jun said. "Because of your archery lesson, my skills will be much improved."

"I will train you again," Woo Jin said. "We have at least four days of travel left. There will be enough time."

Woo Jin indicated the firelance that Ha Jun had packed with the rest of his belongings. "How effective are those? I've heard tales of their power but have never seen one in action."

Ha Jun turned to the weapon strapped to his horse. He stared at it in silence for several moments. "It was given to me at the end of my last quest by the soldier, Seong Min. He said he would have no more need of it. I tried to convince him otherwise, but he was determined to give it to me, and promised that I take it with me on my next quest."

Seong Min, the outgoing and talkative solider who had turned quiet after returning from his journey with Ha Jun. Even with what Ha Jun had spoken about that quest, he hadn't gone into enough specifics. His friend didn't describe what they faced or what had changed the solider so much.

Just as Woo Jin studied the Dark Elf, he had also been studying Ha Jun. Except for that one time in Jeju at the governor's office when his friend had spoken to the Dark Elf in her language, the two had said nothing else to each other. Ha Jun had stayed close to the companions, while Windshine had remained on the periphery, a shadow traveling in their general direction but not one of them. Woo Jin had noticed that, like them, she sneezed because of the pollen in the air. She became congested, her breath whistling through her nose as she struggled to breathe. At night, mosquitoes attacked her just as they attacked the men, and in the morning, he had observed her scratching the bumps the pests left behind.

She ate food that she had brought with her, never sharing their meal with them. He had still not glimpsed her naked, but she would disappear at times, and he guessed it was to relieve herself. Woo Jin became more convinced that her body beneath her clothes was like South Hanguk female bodies. His curiosity still plagued him, however, but the opportunity never came to get a glimpse of her naked.

During their trip together, Woo Jin couldn't help but feel that the Dark Elf was mostly harmless. So why did the government official want her killed? What hidden threat did she pose to the people of South Hanguk?

Woo Jin needed to discover this. It would ease his conscience if he knew why he must assassinate her. If he could just discover what was wrong with her, he would put all doubts from his mind and kill her without hesitation.

He became determined to learn what evil the Dark Elf harbored, and what threat she posed to the county of South Hanguk.

10

The peaks of Seoraksan Mountains pierced the sky as they neared the border.

"We're a day's journey away," In-Su warned them. "There's no stable territory between North and South Hanguk. From this moment on, we must remain vigilant."

Indeed, many of the farmlands had been abandoned; the encircling stonewalls broken, the fields overgrown with tall grass, the weeds choking the life out of plants and vegetables. A constant breeze whistled past scarecrows whose faces had been torn apart by ravens, their eyes missing, their cheeks shredded. From the boughs of trees alongside the road, crows watched the companions pass, their caws as ominous as the smell of decay lingering in the air.

Woo Jin gazed at Seoraksan in awe. In Jeju, nothing could compare to the mountain range's vastness. The inactive volcano at the center of Jeju was a dwarf next to the jagged rock of Seoraksan that stretched to the north for as far as the eye could see.

"We'll stop at dusk to rest," In-Su told them. "The spring has gotten late, and dawn comes early. When we rise, we'll ride with only a short break at midday. We must reach Goseong before nightfall tomorrow. We cannot be caught without shelter so deep within the border after dark."

They were headed east of Seoraksan range, looping back towards the coast of South Hanguk. Goseong wasn't a port city, though rivers ran by it to empty into the sea. In-Su explained what he had heard about the village of children during his deployment on the border.

"The village is surrounded by a mountain range, though they don't rise as high as Seoraksan. Entering Goseong remains difficult to invaders, which is why they lasted so long on the border. Enemies can advance over the mountains, but they're picked off. The Child-God's soldiers are persistent, though. Perhaps by now they've formulated a mode of attack that will lessen their casualties and deliver the women and girls to them."

At dusk, the companions rested and finished off most of their provisions. In-Su told them that they could restock in the village as they prepared the people to be evacuated. He set the watch rotation, and after eating, retired.

The crows quieted. Woo Jin could still make out their dark shapes settled in the branches of trees around them. Their eyes reflected the moonlight, and they maintained a constant vigil on the companions. The monk, Nam Kyu, grasped the golden three-legged crow pendant hanging around his neck and meditated.

When he finished, he warned the group that the crows were searching for souls to carry off to the land of the dead. He echoed In-Su's warning that the companions must be careful. Death reigned in the border between the two warring countries. The land was full of rotted corpses and picked over bones.

When woken for his rotation, Woo Jin took his place on the rough bark of an overturned tree, his hand on the hilt of his sword. He didn't string the bow for fear of weakening its frame. He feared he would need it at full capacity for whatever they faced tomorrow.

Ha Jun took up a position near him. Moments passed, and Ha Jun broke the silence with a solemn, "So this is it."

The simplicity of the pronouncement and what it foreshadowed chilled Woo Jin. His friend stared out at the watching crows, his sword at the ready.

"Tomorrow, we reach the quest's end," Ha Jun continued. "Tomorrow, we see what evil has been waiting for us."

"It may not be so terrible," Woo Jin said. "In-Su seems confident we'll be victorious."

"Yes. I hope he's right."

Ha Jun gave a long, deep sigh. He seemed resigned to some awful fate, and the attitude left Woo Jin frustrated. "You don't want to be here," he said, anger drifting into his voice. "Why did you come? These quests are voluntary."

Ha Jun didn't respond immediately, his brow furrowed as if he struggled to find an answer. A noticeable tremor shook his body. Of fear, Woo Jin wondered. He regarded the hostler yet again. How could someone so strong be so afraid? What exactly had changed him so much during the last quest?

After a few moments Ha Jun admitted, "My father went deep into debt to prepare me for becoming a hero. I cannot disappoint him. I cannot fail."

Woo Jin grew thoughtful at this. The two of them travelled on the quest for the same reasons: family, and more specifically, their fathers, whose expectations they strived to meet.

What was it about fathers and sons that drove men thus? Woo Jin had been trained since childhood to become a hero. The desire to do so felt natural to him now, but how much of it was simply his father trying to live through him?

After their watch, they slept until the early dawn turned the sky a bright blue. The companions had a quick breakfast of squirrel meat and rice, then rode east. Ruins marked the lands within the border. They passed small towns where the people had long ago fled, leaving behind empty homes, thatch roofs fallen in and broken walls covered with vines.

In-Su led the companions down a narrow path that cut through a dense forest. The trees yawned above them, allowing shafts of light to spear the ground through branches heavy with leaves. They rode in silence, taking a short break at midday before pushing forward at In-Su's relentless pace. Their horses neared exhaustion under the humid foliage of the forests, and the companions - thirsty, sweat soaked, and tired - fared little better. When they neared the edge of the tree line, their hearts brightened at the prospect of fresh air despite the coming danger they rode into.

The companions saw that the road dropped out of the forests into wide fields surrounding the village. Light still lingered in the sky, and a nervous excitement spread among them driving away the fatigue. The remnants of farming were visible, though here, too, the land had grown wild. Tall grass reached for the sky, and tattered scarecrows, swaying on wooden poles, dotted the land. Beyond this, the green mountains surrounding the village rose up from the ground. Jutting from the base of the foremost mountain range was a broad red and gold temple with a three-layered slatted roof and a heavily barred gate.

"The entrance to Goseong." Nam-Kyu pointed to the third level of the temple's roof. "Take note of that strange symbol extending from the top. I've never seen anything like it."

If Nam-Kyu hadn't mentioned it, Woo Jin probably wouldn't have seen the two simple white planks. One was embedded vertically in the roof of the temple, and the other intersected it near the top. Nothing seemed particularly special about their configuration, but the unsettled way Nam-Kyu stared at it made Woo Jin wary of the symbol.

"It radiates with an odd spiritual power," the monk said. "It doesn't belong in South Hanguk."

In-Su spared the ornament a brief glance. The path that led through the fields to the temple gate seemed to be of greater importance to him.

Worry etched itself across his brow. "This is why the people of Goseong were able to defend themselves for so long on the border. That road exposes all who travel upon it. An ambush would be simple and devastating."

Kun Woo nodded in agreement. "A fool takes that route. But what other way is there except over the mountains? The traps that lie hidden up there might be even worse. We must travel this path if we want to enter the village of children."

A breeze stirred the grass, bending the stalks towards the coast. Woo Jin felt something, a sense of dread on the wind whispering for them to turn back. And that symbol that left the monk disturbed. It, too, was a bad omen, an object foreign to South Hanguk.

He glanced at the Dark Elf. As always, she stood several paces from them. She gazed at the two white planks on the temple. She knew something about that symbol; he was sure of it. And she probably knew what danger waited for them. Woo Jin wondered if she would watch them walk into a slaughter and do nothing to warn them?

But he already knew the answer to his question. Of course she would. As his elder brother had said, the foreigner wasn't there to interfere. She would simply record their actions, describe the way in which they perished, and return with the report back to the governor of Jeju.

Anger spiked through Woo Jin. She could save their lives, but she would not. Was it wrong to assassinate a foreigner that would watch South Hanguk men die, quest after quest, generation after generation? If he and his companions must fall, did they need those strange blue and brown eyes to watch from a distance and make note of their weakness?

Woo Jin placed his hand upon the pyeonjeons and poison tucked away in his hanbok.

"Four of us will go to the gate," In-Su said. "Ha Jun, Kun Woo, Nam-Kyu, and me. Jae Jin, Ki Ha, Jae Ho, and Woo Jin are to stay in the cover of the forest. You four must understand the absolute importance of your positioning. You must be ready to act at a moment's notice if we fall into trouble." He held the gaze of each of the younger men in turn. "Our lives will be in your hands."

The three brothers readied their instruments. Ki Ha swiveled the drum from his back to his broad chest and tightened the straps around his shoulders. Jae Jin held a long, wooden flute to his lips, his fingers placed over the holes. Jae Ho had brought along two stringed instruments, and chose the haegum, a slender bamboo fiddle with a long neck and a hollow base that he settled against the back of the horse. He placed the bow against the haegum's strings, poised to play at a moment's notice.

Ha Jun poured black powder into the mouth of the firelance, then stuffed a block of bamboo in it so the powder wouldn't spill as he rode. In-Su and Kun Woo slid their swords from their sheaths. Nam-Kyu hooked the fingers of his left hand around the rings of the small knives he carried so that he had three each dangling from his four fingers. Woo Jin couldn't begin to imagine how he planned on using so many of them at one time. He joined the three brothers readying their musical instruments at the very edge of the tree line while the other four companions started slowly down the path.

Out of the corner of his eye, Woo Jin saw the Dark Elf, who stood at the edge of the forest near them. He noticed the way her gaze had become focused, the slight forward tilt of her body as if she anticipated the events that were about to unfold and didn't want to miss anything. He looked to his right and saw the three Jang brothers looking at the four riding forward. It struck Woo Jin that a perfect opportunity to kill the foreigner was about to present itself. But if he made her the target and shot an arrow through her heart now, would he leave his brothers defenseless and potentially allow one of them to be killed?

Woo Jin reached into his hanbok, took a couple of the small pyeonjeons from the folds of his shirt, and allowed his arm sleeve to drape over them.

"The trees above us," Jae Jin said.

Woo Jin started, his heart hammering and his fingers tightening on the arrow shafts at the sudden break in the silence. He steadied his hand and tilted his head up to the branches spawning above them. A sharp gasp escaped his lips. Along the branches, watching the field with tiny black eyes, were dozens of crows. They didn't stir as if they waited for the feast death would soon deliver to them.

Dread filled Woo Jin, and he directed his attention back to the path leading through the fields. To protect his brothers or to slay the foreigner? Loyalty to his companions or devotion to his family? In a split second, he may be forced to decide, and he couldn't make up his mind as to which choice was better than the other.

The four companions struggled with the reins when their mounts began to wildly shake their heads. Panicked neighing floated back to the forest as the horses kicked the dirt and tried to backtrack down the path towards the tree line. Their riders' steady hands brought them under control. Woo Jin saw his brothers turn their attention to the tall grass bending in the steady breeze blowing east across the land.

An earsplitting screech erupted from the temple. The gate rose. Woo Jin clenched his teeth at the awful, grinding sound. He expected a horde of shadowy figures to rush out of the temple and attack his brothers. The breeze became a sudden gale that set the scare-crows spinning round on their poles in a macabre dance.

A young woman dashed out of the gate. Her long black hair whipped across her shoulders. Woo Jin stared at her in amazement. The fullness of her body, her shapely hips, the perfection of her face, pale and round. He marveled at the beauty that radiated from her and caught him in its brilliant grasp.

In a clear voice that carried across the fields to the

trees, the woman yelled to the four companions on the road, "They're out there waiting for you. Run!"

The scarecrows sank into the ground, then erupted upwards. A shower of dirt and clumps of earth exploded into the air. North Hanguk soldiers clambered out of trenches hidden by the grass and rushed the companions. The crows leapt from the trees in a clamor of sharp caws and circled like a black cloud above the killing fields. Ha Jun uncorked his firelance, lit the end of it, and aimed at the advancing soldiers. A dagger flung from a swift hand spun through the air and slammed into his chest, burying itself to the hilt. With a cry, Ha Jun slipped from his horse as the wick of the lance hit the powder. A burst of flame shot from the weapon's metal mouth to set the grass on fire.

The cloud of circling crows let loose a chorus of staccato bursts as if the black birds laughed in glee at the first victim of the melee. In-Su and Kun Woo rode forward and lashed out at soldiers who tried to leap upon the fallen Ha Jun and hack away at him with blades glinting orange in the sunlight.

Nam-Kyu threw his knives into air and grabbed the golden medallion around his neck. A space near the monk rippled, then became translucent as it spread outward. A spectral figure with several contorting faces materialized out of the tear in reality and unfolded thin tentacles from around its body. The entity looped its many arms through the rings of the blades and flung itself forward like a cyclone, spinning the knives round and round and cutting through chain mail, flesh, and bone of the attacking soldiers.

"Woo Jin," Jae Jin yelled. "Ride forward and let the music take you!" He placed the flute to his lips and blew a long, continuous note that seeded life in Woo Jin and caused the world to sharpen with startlingly clarity. Jae Ho plucked the strings of the fiddle with successive flicks of his wrist, and Woo Jin's heartbeat quickened as he snapped the reins and set the horse charging down the path. He slipped the pyeonjeons into the quiver as he grabbed a longer arrow and nocked it. When Ki Ha struck the drum, the blow rumbled across the field like thunder, and confidence filled and electrified Woo Jin like a bolt of lightning. He released the first arrow; it soared fast and true and struck a solider through the throat. He nocked and released a second, and a third, his hands moving faster than he could think as the waves of the music merged him into perfect unity with his killer instinct.

North Hanguk soldiers fell one after the other under the barrage from his bow. Woo Jin crouched on the back of his galloping horse and picked off another solider with an arrow through the eye, then another. In-Su dismounted as the enemy fell back and tried to lift Ha Jun onto the back of the horse. Surprise and desperation filled his cries for help, as Ha Jun proved too heavy to move. Kun Woo dismounted, and together they hefted a slumped Ha Jun on the back of his horse.

Woo Jin, down to the last four of his two dozen long arrows, had felled twenty North Hanguk soldiers with a single strike each. The rest were retreating, zigzagging across the grass in a desperate attempt to avoid his perfect aim. One of them placed a horn to his lips, but Woo Jin let loose his twenty-first arrow.

Without pausing, another soldier snatched up the horn from his comrade's lifeless fingers, placed it to his lips, and blew a note that roared through the mountains. An arrow that went through his spine into his heart cut it short, but the echoes of the horn blast bounced around the mountainside for some time before they finally died.

Horror transfixed the girl's majestic face. She urged the companions to join her at the gate. As Woo Jin rode past the trenches where the North Hanguk soldiers had been hiding, the overwhelming stench of rotting flesh made him gag. This must have been what spooked the horses. There were so many corpses that Woo Jin couldn't count them. They were not only North Hanguk soldiers. South Hanguk men lay among them, dismembered, the ground dark beneath them.

Woo Jin reached the temple gates alongside In-Su, Kun Woo, and Nam-Kyu. Ha Jun, slung over his horse, was gasping for air, his blood soaking the flanks of his horse. The champions of the spirit caught up with them moments later.

The girl rushed to Ha Jun. As she inspected him, she said to the others over her shoulder, "We don't have much time. That solider has signaled for reinforcements. Many more will come before long. Each time this has happened, they've doubled their number. It could be more than five dozen next time."

Sixty North Hanguk soldiers? How would the seven of them fight so many while evacuating Goseong?

Ha Jun had spoken true. Death had been waiting for them. Now that they had rushed into its embrace, it would wrap cold fingers around their throats, strangle the life out of them, and feed their cold bodies to the laughing crows wheeling in black clouds over their heads.

11

When the companions exited the tunnel leading from the gate into Goseong, they saw young boys standing alongside young girls. Anyone who appeared to be in their teens or older, however, was female.

The villagers waited at the end of the tunnel and gathered around Woo Jin and his brothers as they dismounted. Both In-Su and Kun Woo were needed to take the heavy Ha Jun from his horse. Blood soaked, the hostler's hanbok was dark red, his skin ashen, his eyes closed. He did not stir. The monk knelt beside him, placed his fingers against Ha Jun's neck and wrist, then held his palm in front of Ha Jun's nose. Above them, the crows circled in a cackling vortex of flapping wings and black feathers.

"They're searching for his soul." Nam-Kyu took hold of the three-legged crow medallion in both hands.

"I will try and locate his spirit before the birds find it and take him to the next life."

The girl who had led them through the temple gates also knelt beside Ha Jun. Woo Jin's breath caught in his throat at her beauty. Her long black hair flowed down her slender shoulders to her shapely waist. Woo Jin studied her round face, taking in her enticing eyes, full lashes, parted red lips. His gaze travelled down the graceful slope of her neck to rest upon her firm breasts stretching against the simple hanbok she wore. Heat suffused Woo Jin, and he swallowed in a throat gone dry as he resisted an urge to caress her.

To distract himself from the pressure exerting from his loins, Woo Jin directed his gaze to the necklace settled between her breasts. It was the same as the one atop the temple. The ornament dangled above Ha Jun as she knelt over him, her eyes closed. She clasped her palms together, the fingers of both hands interlocked and folded over each other. A series of words in a language Woo Jin had never heard came to her lips. The monk, still grasping the golden medallion, stared in curiosity at her. When a soft light emanated from her, the monk stepped back in amazement.

"She's communing with *something*," he said in awe, his eyes darting around as if he searched the invisible ether. "Whatever it is, its presence is incredible!"

Woo Jin saw nothing but felt something warm with the consistency of water rising up around him to submerge his body in its presence. He couldn't tear his gaze from the girl, who became even more irresistible as the light around her brightened.

Ha Jun gasped for several breaths of air and his eyes opened.

The women and children gathered around the companions all spoke a word that Woo Jin could not understand: *Ah Men*.

"He must rest," the girl said, exhausted. She struggled to stand, but her knees gave out from under her. Woo Jin rushed to her, hands outstretched. She took them with a smile. Using him as support, she regained her footing. The nearness of her body created a piercing ache in Woo Jin, the need for release making him tremble.

"I saw you on the fields protecting your brothers," the girl said. "Your strength was incredible! I've never seen anything like it."

The compliment made Woo Jin so lightheaded that he wondered if he would float into the sky and be whisked away by the crows into the realm of the dead.

In-Su stepped forward. "Woo Jin is one of Jeju's best warriors. None can compare to him on the island."

The girl's eyes shone like tiny stars upon Woo Jin. She tightened her grip on his hands. Woo Jin wished she would never release him.

"My name is Hwang Ji Su. I'm happy you came to us. We're in desperate need of the best!" She looked at the women and young children gathered around them. "The warriors of Goseong weren't supposed to be gone long when the Emperor summoned them to help with the fortifications in Seoraksan Mountains, but months have passed and they haven't return. A garrison of retired soldiers and inexperienced men remained to protect the village, but when the North Hanguk soldiers laid siege, the supplies ran out, and the men sacrificed themselves to save us from starvation."

Grief traced lines across the faces of the villagers. Ji Su added, "We watched our brothers and grandfathers be slaughtered so that we would live."

Woo Jin heard sniffles amongst the youngest children, but there were no tears. Those must have been shed long ago.

"And the grandmothers?" In-Su asked. He looked from face to face amongst those gathered. "I don't see them here."

Ji Su bit her lip and glanced at the surrounding young ones. Leaning close to In-Su, she said in a hushed voice, "As long as a little one was hungry or thirsty, they refused to eat or drink what little provisions were left." She shook her head. "They, too, are gone."

In-Su nodded with a deep sigh. "Then we must concentrate upon the living, and make sure the sacrifices of the elders weren't in vain. You said there would be North Hanguk reinforcements? How long do you think before they come?"

"It never takes long," Ji Su replied. "Before tomorrow night."

"Then if we are to evacuate the village," In-Su said, "we must do so soon."

Nam-Kyu stepped forward. "Ha Jun has been brought back to life, but he must rest. There are also many children that we must consider. We must prepare them for the day's march south away from the border."

"I know." In-Su motioned to Ha Jun. "Let's move him into one of the houses."

Kun Woo bent down beside Ha Jun, unbuckled the sword, and tried to pick it up. His eyes opened wide as he struggled to lift the weapon off the ground. It was only with tremendous effort, both arms straining and his legs quivering, that he managed to heft the sword up.

"It's incredible!" he breathed out in awe. "How does he wield it?'

The monk came forward and studied it. "Look at the inscriptions there." He pointed to the hilt. "This wasn't made by human hands. It's a glyph sword, crafted by the dark elves."

Woo Jin had lost track of Windshine up until that moment. Now he scanned the area. He was surprised to discover that she had managed to enter Goseong and stood at the edge of the crowd of villagers. Several nearby children looked at her curiously. One, a little girl only a few years old, reached out and took the foreigner's hand. Windshine looked down at the child, an unreadable expression sweeping her features. Woo Jin couldn't guess how Windshine would react, but she didn't step away from the little girl, nor did she withdraw her hand.

With the sword removed, In-Su carried Ha Jun to the nearest house. The homes of Goseong were constructed in the typical fashion of South Hanguk dwellings, with stone walls and thatch roofs. In-Su laid Ha Jun on a sleeping mat.

"He will need food and water," Nam Kyu said.

Several children ran off, and returned with a bowl of rice, strips of dried pork, and a basin of clear water.

"We don't have much, but he will need his strength returned as soon as possible," Ji Su said. "He will be of some use to you all, won't he?"

Kun Woo had dragged Ha Jun's sword into the house and dropped it beside him. "We haven't seen him in combat," he said, "but he should be of use. The governor wouldn't have sent him on this quest if he wasn't worthy."

They stepped outside, leaving Ha Jun to rest.

"How many people are left in the village?" In-Su asked.

"A hundred and thirteen," Ji Su responded. "Before the Emperor called up our soldiers, there were 324 of us. Ninety-three of our men went to help with the fortifications. They were happy to serve the Emperor, but they worried about leaving their families behind. The Emperor's messenger had assured them it would only be a short deployment."

Sadness weighed down Ji Su's words. Woo Jin wanted to wrap his arms around her and tell her that everything would be okay. The Emperor only called up village men when the standing army was stretched thin. There would be many South Hanguk fighters working together, which improved the odds that any attack by the north would be repelled.

"Six months ago," Ji Su said, "the North Hanguk soldiers came. In the borderlands, we know they are looking for women to kidnap, and we've always been careful. There were only a small number of the northern soldiers, and our grandfathers held off that first wave as they tried to enter Goseong over the mountains. But when double the number came as reinforcements, they started a siege. We had enough provisions to last through the summer, but then the winter came. The grandfathers rationed the food, but the stores still dropped, and they didn't know when the soldiers of Goseong would return to drive the enemy away so we could start farming the fields beyond the gate again." Ji Su paused and glanced around at the nearby children. She lowered her voice when she added, "As the months passed, they began to wonder if our men would ever come back home."

"Seoraksan has many strange dangers," In-Su admitted. "There might have been a greater conflict there than first anticipated. If that is true, the war may be pushing further south of the border."

"The grandfathers said the same," Ji Su said. "They didn't think we could afford to wait and decided to face the enemy themselves. Our brothers insisted on joining them. They'd been trained by our fathers but had never been in a real battle before. The grandfathers and our brothers planned an attack that they thought had the greatest chance of success, but the Child-God's warriors were too powerful. They slaughtered all of them and dumped their bodies in the fields before the temple gate."

"Did the North Hanguk soldiers try and storm the village again?" In-Su asked.

Ji Su nodded. "They did, but the women aren't completely unskilled in defense. Like the men, we know the mountains and their traps. The North Hanguk soldiers retreated to the fields, and now they're trying to starve us out. It wouldn't have been much longer before we had no choice but to be taken by them and brought back to bear children for the Child-God's men."

"We will do everything we can to get you and the young ones out of here without harm," In-Su said. "We won't have to travel far, but it is a full day's journey."

"An entire day." Ji Su regarded the children. Many had gathered around the Dark Elf, who gazed out north, though all there was to see were the surrounding mountains. Still, it seemed like she was watching something far away unfold, her eyes focused on the distance.

"The young ones are weak from rationing, and a day's march will seem a great journey to them. They haven't often travelled away from Goseong. Most of them have never been further than the farming fields outside the temple."

"I understand," In-Su said, "but there's no other way. The children must eat what they can tonight, for we'll travel light. And they must rest. We leave at dawn. Hopefully, the North Hanguk reinforcements will still be far off when we set out."

The monk stepped forward. "What is that symbol you wear around your neck? I've never seen anything like it."

A serene smile spread Ji Su's lips. "It's beautiful, isn't it? It comes from the western world. Foreigners came to Goseong two years ago. They said they were preaching something called the Gospel. They taught us about their god, Hana-Nim. They said that there is great love in Hana-Nim's teachings, and that we should follow them. That if the people of South and North Hanguk followed His teachings, we could end the war between us."

Nam-Kyu's eyes narrowed as Ji Su spoke. Woo Jin didn't like what he saw in his elder brother's face. Concern for Ji Su burrowed its way into him, and his desire to protect her from harm deepened.

The monk turned to In-Su. "Foreigners somehow slipped past the guards at the ports into the interior of South Hanguk? I wonder if the Emperor is aware of this."

"We'll have to inform the governor when we return to Jeju," In-Su replied. "I'm sure the westerners can't still be in South Hanguk. They would have certainly been detained by now."

Ji Su looked from the monk, to the soldier, and back at the monk again in confusion. "They weren't dangerous," she insisted. "Hana-Nim has kept the village safe as we held out through the cold months with the North Hanguk men right outside the temple gates waiting to steal us away." She clasped her hands together in the strange way that she had done earlier when she knelt over Ha Jun and restored him to life. "It was through Hana-Nim that I was able to save your friend. You must believe me, Hana-Nim is peace and love. There's nothing bad in His teachings."

Ji Su's attempts to persuade the monk seemed to have an opposite effect, his face hardening at her defense.

"Evil comes in many forms," he lectured her, his

voice harsh and tinged with impatience. "Societies strive to create order so that all may live knowing what is right and what is wrong. That is what we call harmony. When outside elements are allowed to enter, balance is threatened. Without balance, societies are thrown into chaos. Chaos brings hardships when people no longer know their proper place in the world. Hardships bring misery. Misery breeds hatred. Out of hatred, conflict flourishes."

He pointed to the ornament around Ji Su's neck. "You wear that without knowing the history of it or its effects on those who have heard this Gospel. You speak of Hana-Nim's words, but words can be interpreted in a myriad of ways. Sometimes for good, sometimes for evil, no matter their original intent. You use the power of Hana-Nim without knowing the exact price you are paying for its bounty."

To In-Su, the monk said, "The Emperor must learn of this. The matter will have to be settled later."

In-Su agreed. "What is of greater importance now is completing the quest and evacuating Goseong. We will need arrows for Woo Jin. Take him to your armory," he told Ji Su, "and retrieve all of them that you can find. In order to save Goseong, we must use Woo Jin as our greatest weapon."

With that, In-Su and Nam-Kyu joined the other brothers, leaving Woo Jin and Ji Su alone.

12

Tears sparkled at the edges of Ji Su's eyes. Woo Jin wanted to brush them away, but he didn't know how to touch her in such an intimate manner. Ji Su's every emotion fueled a fire burning inside of him. Her every gesture seemed like magic. He struggled not to forget the quest, not to forget his brothers and family, not to forget the war between the North and South, not to forget everything and simply lose himself in her.

"They're wrong." Ji Su looked at Woo Jin, and his heart ached at the ferocity of her grief. "There is nothing dangerous in His words."

Woo Jin wished he could comfort her by agreeing with her beliefs, but the words didn't materialize. Like the monk, he rejected the idea of foreigners wandering South Hanguk. They must have known that it was against the wishes of the Emperor. All who dock at the ports are made aware of this decree. Yet the foreigners had disobeyed the will of the land, snuck past the many guards patrolling the harbor, and spread their teachings to the people of South Hanguk at their discretion. Just the subterfuge by itself gave doubt to the purity of their motives.

But the sorrow that brushed Ji Su's beauty at Nam-Kyu's harsh words touched Woo Jin. He wanted her to be happy; he wanted to fill her with joy.

He asked, "Will you show me the store of weapons? As I said before, I promise to do everything within my power to keep the children of Goseong alive."

Ji Su seemed reluctant to leave the subject behind, so Woo Jin added, "While we walk, will you tell me about Hana-Nim? I would love to learn more about Him."

Ji Su's expression brightened. She nodded with enthusiasm and said, "Come with me. I'll take you to the armory."

They walked down the main lane of the village. The voices of Woo Jin's elder brothers formulating tomorrow's strategy, and the children chatting around Windshine, fell away, so that Woo Jin was able to get his wish. He and Ji Su were alone.

The sun was setting behind the horizon. Its dying light smeared the pale clouds hovering above the mountains in bright orange and red hues. The crows had finally quieted, no longer visible in the sky. This far north, a crisp wind had picked up and swept through the trees. The icy fingers of the mountains invaded the folds of Woo Jin's hanbok and stung his skin. Shivering, he noticed that Ji Su didn't seem effected by it.

"Hana-Nim walked the world once," Ji Su began. "He was born in a land far, far away, in a time long ago. His mother was a simple woman and laid with Hana-Nam to bear Him into the world."

"He laid with her to bear himself into the world?" Woo Jin asked, confused. "How is that possible?"

"Hana-Nim isn't actually one, but three. The Father, the Son, and the Holy Spirit."

The explanation didn't clear the matter up for Woo Jin. "He is three? Where does he live?"

Ji Su pointed up at the blue sky darkening to twilight. "Hana-Nim exists above us in a land of pure happiness and love. In His realm, there is no suffering, there is no want. He looks down upon us judging our actions. Those who live by His word will return to Him, for He created the world and all that exists inside of it."

The idea of an afterlife without conflict intrigued Woo Jin. The spirit world that South Hanguk people believed in wasn't an existence of peace. Trials existed there because through struggle, greater wisdom and strength could be attained. In Hana-Nim's realm, if there was only peace, how did the souls continue to improve? Without tests, how could they reach greater states of awareness?

"When the Hana-Nim was born," Ji Su continued, "He walked throughout His country teaching about His Father's message of forgiveness. He comforted the sick and fed the hungry."

Ji Su's story made little sense to Woo Jin. If Hana-Nim was a Lord, like the Emperor of South Hanguk, why would He walk amongst the poor? Wouldn't that be the duty of His attendants? And if He ruled His country, how did He find the time to travel across the ocean to their land?

"Was He the one who came to Goseong?" he asked her.

Ji Su laughed. "No, of course not! Hana-Nim died a long time ago. He sacrificed Himself for our *ɔin-ɔuh*." She spoke the last word in the foreign language she had used when she saved Ha Jun.

"Our *ɔin-ɔuh*? What does that mean?"

"We have something called original *ɔin-ɔuh*. This is the curse that comes with being born. It encourages us to do evil instead of good and makes returning to Hana-Nim's land of pure happiness impossible. This is man's terrible burden, for those who do evil end up *ðown there*."

Ji Su's voice dropped to a hushed whisper, her face twisting in terror as she pointed down. "That's where demons live. When souls go there, they're tortured for all time."

Woo Jin gazed down at the ground and tried to imagine the reality Ji Su described. The idea of endless torture horrified him. A philosophy that taught eternal suffering without a chance of redemption seemed need-lessly cruel. So this was what the foreigners had taught the people of Goseong? The monk, Nam-Kyu, would grow ever more suspicious should he learn the truth of Hana-Nim's teachings.

They reached a long, rectangular building near the edge of the village. Ji Su led Woo Jin inside, and he immediately saw that the armory was almost empty. A few swords hung from racks on the walls. There were several pole arms, an axe, and two wide barrels of arrows. Woo Jin went to them and counted forty altogether. Beyond that, the armory seemed like it hadn't been used in many weeks, if not months.

"We've gone through most of the stores," Ji Su said. "First the fathers, then the grandfathers and brothers, and finally us women when we were all that was left."

Looking over the depleted armory, Woo Jin couldn't help but marvel that the remaining villagers had repelled the North Hanguk soldiers. The ornament around Ji Su's neck caught his eye, and a sudden realization dawned over him. If the foreigners possessed the power of whatever that symbol represented, then they could cause much havoc in South Hanguk. What if they still wandered the country? If the Emperor exerted His full might upon them, they of course would fall. But how many of the converted country's people would have to be sacrificed in order to stamp out the believers in Hana-Nim?

The monk was right. When balance was threatened, conflict followed close behind.

Ji Su staring at him broke Woo Jin's musings. His flesh warmed as heat swept through his body. Again, her beauty pierced him. He cleared his throat and glanced down, but he felt her eyes still on him and caught her gaze again. A violent tremble ran down his spine and spread out along his arms and legs. Ji Su approached Woo Jin, and his breath caught in his throat. A stinging pain welled up inside of him, a longing that he couldn't explain swelling his chest such that he feared he would burst open in front of her.

When Ji Su took his hands again in her small, gentle ones, Woo Jin froze, all moments of his past and all potential paths of his future disappearing leaving only this present reality of exquisite torture to exist.

"Please, protect us," Ji Su said, drifting closer to him.

"I've already promised you that." Woo Jin's reply came out as a strangled gasp harsh in his ears. The nearness of her body increased the threat of explosion. His legs weakened under the building pressure and he feared toppling over and rumbling the earth with his fall. Perspiration broke out over his feverish flesh despite the chill wind of the north. The shirt and pants of his hanbok clung to him, plastered to his flesh with sweat.

"You did," Ji Su agreed in the same gentle tones as if she was unaware of the distress the scent of her hair and the warmth of her body caused him. Space between them shrank further though she did not seem to move, leaving Woo Jin longing for this pained moment to end and deliver him from his suffering.

"The children of Goseong need a protector," Ji Su said. "The women of Goseong need a leader." Her mouth hovered near his. Her breath touched his lips and Woo Jin gave a low groan, his heart bucking against his chest in a wild effort to break his ribs and escape into her embrace.

And then her last words to him, spoken with heart-felt earnestness. "Woo Jin. Will you be our protector, our leader? Will you become my savior?"

Her request speared through him. He could withstand no more. Distance between them ceased to exist, and their bodies pressed together as they kissed. Thoughts scrambled away from Woo Jin. Reality fell away to be replaced by a consuming desire for Ji Su that swallowed him whole.

13

Woo Jin and Ji Su's shoulders brushed against each other as they carried the arrows back to the temple gates. They set the barrels in front of In-Su, who frowned.

"So that was all that was left?" he asked. The children of Goseong stopped speaking at the grim tone of his voice. "Woo Jin, you'll have to make every arrow count. We'll have none to waste on the enemy."

All eyes focused on Woo Jin. He strode forward and said in a loud, clear voice, "Each pull of the string will be the death of a North Hanguk soldier. On my own, I will kill forty. No child here will come to harm at the hands of the enemy. This, I promise!"

Woo Jin had never felt so alive as he did at this moment. His purpose was clear. He would be the man Ji Su envisioned and save the children of her village. He would lead them from the border to safety without allowing harm to come to even one of them. Fire burned hot inside of him. Like the volcano in the center of Jeju, Woo Jin had erupted. He was no longer a child, but an adult. The world would witness the raw power that he alone possessed, and they would roar his name and proclaim him a hero.

In-Su, standing before Woo Jin, glanced at Ji Su, the ends of his lips curving upwards in a small smile. He then turned to the champions of the spirit, the three Jang brothers.

"Your music will have to be focused wider this time, upon all of us," he said, to which Ki Ha nodded.

"It will be so," the oldest of the three siblings assured In-Su. "But while we spread our music to a wider audience, we won't be able to fight, or defend ourselves. Someone will have to protect us as we ride beside you should the enemy overtake us."

"I know." In-Su rubbed his bearded chin. "It will be imperative for Woo Jin to take out as many of the enemy from a distance as possible. If any of the north-erners break through his barrage, it will be up to me, Kun Woo, and Nam-Kyu to protect the flanks of the villagers. There are so many children, and so few of us." In-Su sighed. "I don't know if he'll be ready, but Ha Jun will have to fight whether he's recovered or not."

Kun Woo shook his head. "It won't be enough. We need more."

The monk stepped forward. "I can give you more. It will take great energy from me, so I also will not be able to fight alongside you. But we can honor the grandfa-thers of Goseong by giving them another chance. I can summon their spirits back to their bodies of flesh so that they can fight alongside us and protect their women and children in this land of the living."

"Is such a thing possible?" In-Su gasped.

Nam-Kyu nodded. "Our ancestors watch over us in the realm they inhabit. In that place, they have their own trials, their own hardships, but their love for their bloodlines keep them connected to the living. It is why we pray to them and keep memorials for them. To keep strong the bridge between the past and the present, between the living and the dead."

As the monk spoke, a look of horror filled Ji Su's face. She shook her head, her long black hair whipping around her face. "No, no, no!"

She rushed forward, her protests a wail that silenced the startled soldier and monk.

"No!"

Some of the youngest of Goseong started to cry, and their older siblings held on tight to them.

"You can't steal the souls of our grandfathers and brothers from Hana-Nim's paradise! They have already sacrificed themselves. It was His will that they died so that we could live. You can't dishonor that and force them back to their rotting corpses."

The monk's look of confusion darkened to anger as Ji Su explained to him exactly what she had told Woo Jin.

"Enough of this western nonsense!" he roared at her. "The souls of your grandfathers would not spend their eternity in some foreign entity's reality." He spat on the ground at Ji Su's feet. "These are South Hanguk men. They were born here, grew up here, married here, birthed children here, and died here. Their blood soaks the land of our country, not the land of some country across the sea. Those men knew their duty to our people, and even in death they will hold true to it."

Ji Su clasped her hands together. "You don't understand! There is only one Creator, and souls return to Him if they are deemed worthy. Everything else comes from *there*!" She stomped her foot on the ground. "Everything else is wrong!"

"But you brought Ha Jun back from the dead," In-Su said. "Didn't you take his soul from this Hana-Nim?"

"You can only join Hana-Nim after the *ceremony of water*. If that doesn't happen, your soul goes to a different place. A place without rest, a place without light. A place of *always waiting without end*. You are denied entrance to Paradise without the *ceremony of water*!"

Woo Jin went rigid at the rage that contorted the monk's face. That look was a hair's breadth from violence. If Nam-Kyu struck Ji Su, Woo Jin couldn't stand there and do nothing. Yet how could he fight his elder brother? How could he raise a hand to his companion?

He wanted to share Ji Su's concern, but without the aid of the dead grandfathers, how would they evacuate the children of Goseong? Woo Jin knew he could fell a soldier with a single arrow, but that would only be forty northerners. What if Ji Su was right, and at least a hundred came as reinforcements? What would Woo Jin do about another sixty highly trained North Hanguk warriors?

"Enough." In-Su stepped towards Ji Su. "You're a woman, and a child. The foreign teachings have made you forget your place," he said, towering over her. "We are men, and we're twice your age. You'll be silent from this point onward, and you will simply obey us."

In-Su gestured around him. "We won't allow the slaughter of these children because of the silly beliefs of distant lands. Tomorrow at dawn, we ride from this village. For your sake, and for the sake of these children who rely upon you, do nothing to hinder us. It's our quest to rescue this village, and we'll use every resource we can to ensure success."

His eyes narrowed upon Ji Su. "Nothing will stop us from carrying out our duties, as prescribed by the governor of Jeju."

Without waiting for Ji Su to respond, In-Su turned away from her to the watching children. "You must eat now, and then go to sleep," he instructed them. "Tomorrow will be very dangerous, but we will keep you safe. As South Hanguk men, it is our sacred obligation to protect the next generation of our mighty people."

Ji Su's body shook but when she started to speak again, a soft melody floated from Jae Jin's flute, accompanied by the pluck of the strings from Jae Ho's fiddle. Under the music, tension drained away from Woo Jin, but it was Ji Su who seemed most effected by it. She stumbled, her eyes closing to half slits as she struggled to maintain her footing. She couldn't resist the magic in the music directed at her, and she collapsed. Woo Jin rushed forward and caught her in his arms before she hit the ground.

The anger in Nam-Kyu's face became softened by the tune, but Woo Jin still saw the fire in his eyes as he gazed at Ji Su. Nothing could steal away the grave concern that blossomed inside of Woo Jin for this girl he had vowed to protect only a short while ago.

He could say nothing in front of his elder brothers, but in his heart, he was still her savior. He would do anything to serve her, no matter the costs to honor, or duty. Or his life.

14

The only ones who managed to sleep were the children. In-Su had ordered them to pull their mats from their homes and place them around the mouth of the tunnel so that they would be ready to start off when they awoke.

The fire that had erupted inside of Woo Jin cooled, and as the night wore on, doubts crept in to chill his soul. He tried to ignore the even breathing of the young ones as he checked his weapons over once, then again. The rhythmic sound of innocent bliss from the children's small noses and puckered lips made his throat constrict. He had promised to protect them, but those words were easy to say with the warm body of Ji Su by his side. Now he sat without her, surrounded by the most vulnerable of war-torn South Hanguk people who, nevertheless, slept peacefully because they had faith in the companions who had come to rescue them. They couldn't imagine the bleak reality they all faced tomorrow.

Woo Jin again saw the dagger spinning through the air to slam into Ha Jun's chest, the blood that pumped from his body to stain his hanbok dark red. The northerners tomorrow would be relentless in their attempts to kill the companions and steal the women and girls away.

If there was any consolation in the children sleeping around Woo Jin, it was that they couldn't witness his lack of confidence at the thought of saving them from the clutches of the Child-God and the North Hanguk soldiers.

Worst of all, Woo Jin worried about Ji Su. He yearned to keep his promise to her more than anything else. He cast his eyes to where she slumbered far from him on the other side of the young ones. The spell the brothers had put her under was potent, yet she turned and twisted in her sleep as she wrestled with dark and terrible dreams. Unlike him, she didn't have the ability stay awake from the terrors brought upon by nightmares.

It was because of this imprisonment within her mind by the melody of the music that Woo Jin wanted to hold her in his arms. He couldn't bear thinking about how awful it would be to dwell in horrifying dreams one could not break free from.

Gathering his courage, he set his weapons aside, picked up his mat, and brought it next to her so that he could lie down beside her. Before he could do so, Kun

Woo, the bearded soldier, walked over and stepped in between them.

"She'll be fine."

Woo Jin looked away from the knowing grin curving Kun Woo's lips, and hoped the heat that flushed his face wasn't visible.

"I just want to make sure," Woo Jin responded, unable to meet his elder brother's eye.

Kun Woo guffawed. "Your heart is in the right place, but your body isn't to be trusted."

With a firm grip, he led Woo Jin back away from Ji Su. "There's weakness of the flesh in your eyes, little brother. You would dishonor her, and yourself, before the night is over."

The urge to persuade the old soldier to let him stay surged through him. He wanted to offer Kun Woo any number of promises. He would insist that he wouldn't touch Ji Su inappropriately no matter how much his fingers remembered the supple texture of her skin and the burning heat of her body. He would just settle next to her, brush the hair from her beautiful face and soothe the nightmares entrapping her in her unnatural sleep.

He wished to convince Kun Woo that he didn't notice Ji Su's breasts pushed firmly against the shirt of her hanbok, or her full, slightly parted lips, the alluring swell of her hips beckoning him, or the sweet aroma of her sweat that had wrapped itself around him when he'd caught her from falling, and still lingered on his clothes now.

Kun Woo, though, had an expression in his eyes that reminded Woo Jin of his father. There would be no changing his mind on the subject, so Woo Jin would be forced to wait until she awakened from the spell so he could rush to her. He would be the first sight she saw once the music released her from its clutches.

Woo Jin settled his mat far from her and tried to sleep. Every time he closed his eyes, he glimpsed fractured visions of Goseong's children, moaning, dying, dismembered, blood spilling from gaping wounds and coloring the wet earth black: dead; flies popping off tongues distended from mouths opened wide in final screams of anguish: bloated.

These phantoms billowed up from the swirling darkness behind his lids. Nam-Kyu came to him for the night watch and led him and Jae Jin up a narrow trail to the top of the mountains. There, he pointed out one of many sentry posts hidden in the trees. Woo Jin climbed up a rope ladder and settled onto the wooden perch, his eyes directed north. Jae Jin took another position some distance away, leaving Woo Jin alone in silence.

Jae Ho and Ki Ha came to replace them some time later. Woo Jin shuddered at the thought of attempting to sleep once more. When he returned to his mat, he unsheathed his swords, took up a whetstone, and began to sharpen them in long, even strokes.

In-Su approached. "You can't do this now. You already checked your weapons. Rest."

Woo Jin didn't want to meet his elder brother's gaze. He didn't want the worry and fear about the coming morning to show, revealing his weakness.

In-Su laid a hand on his shoulder. "I know what

you're thinking. I know what you see when you close your eyes. It's the same for all of us. Look around you."

Woo Jin followed In-Su's gaze to his brothers lying down on their separate mats. They, too, were restless, turning over on the ground and staring up at the stars blanketing the sky. The moon, caring not for their troubles, bathed the village in a ghostly pale light.

"We're all trying to rest, but for you, it's most important that you are ready. You're our key tomorrow. No one has your skill with the bow, and we must take out as many of the enemy as we can before they reach the children." In-Su squeezed Woo Jin's shoulder. "We need you at your most alert. That won't happen if you don't try and rest."

Woo Jin nodded, though he didn't think sleep would come to him. He lay down, and In-Su retreated. He shut his eyes, and the visions of failure rushed up out of the darkness to plague him once more.

Before dawn, Ki Ha tapped Woo Jin on the shoulder and beckoned him to join the other companions huddled together in the mouth of the tunnel. Four of them stood around a small coal fire, a deep, wide tin pail rested over the flames. The simmering liquid inside was dark yellow and thick, an acrid smell rising with the steam and making Woo Jin's eyes water.

"After we eat, I will administer a small dose to each of the villagers," Nam-Kyu explained. "It'll give them the energy they'll need to push forward without rest for the day's march."

He held up the ladle to Ki Ha. "We will take a dose twice as much as theirs," Nam-Kyu explained. "The first now, the second before we leave. This special ginseng is for emergencies only. It gives the body energy but damages the organs. It takes years off a person's life if consumed often."

Ki Ha took the ladle and swallowed a draught of the liquid. His face reddened as harsh coughs wracked his body. Each of them had the same reaction. When Woo Jin swallowed the ginseng, it tore at his mouth, and he coughed in a vain effort to mitigate the feeling of tiny grains shredding apart his throat. The tonic generated a heat that spread out from his stomach into his arms, legs, up to his head, and down to his feet.

"Ha Jun?" Jae Jin gasped. "Where is he?"

"Still resting." Ki Ha wiped the tears from his eyes and the mucous dripping from his nose with the sleeve of his hanbok.

"I will add something extra to his so that he can operate despite his injury," the monk said. "He will pay a heavy physical price for it one day, but we need that sacrifice of him now."

In-Su, who had taken the last shift in the post amongst the trees, rushed into the tunnel as light from the dawning sun touched the dark sky.

"We must wake the children," he said. "At the horizon are shifting shadows scarring the land. It must be the North Hanguk soldiers marching upon us under the cover of darkness."

"The Child-God's magic," the monk said. "They want to hide their numbers until the last possible moment."

"Well, that moment has arrived," In-Su said. "We

must give everything we have to save the women and children, for their fates at the hands of the northern men would be most terrible."

Woo Jin's jaw clenched at the idea of the northern men having their way with Ji Su. All of the girls who were of childbearing age would be impregnated as quickly as possible so they would not try to escape. The northern men would wait a few years for the youngest ones to mature before it would be their turn to give birth to males, as the Child-God wished. And of course, the young boys of the village would be slaughtered and left to rot in the surrounding fields.

"We cannot allow ourselves to fail them," In-Su said. "Today, we face death with open eyes and brave hearts."

He extended his hand, and one by one the brothers laid their palms on top of his and said in unison, "With open eyes and brave hearts, we fight into our graves."

15

A long, shrill cry sliced through the early morning quiet of the camp. The brothers dashed out of the tunnel to the children and saw Ji Su, awake and on her feet, her eyes wild.

"You can't call the grandfathers back from Paradise," she howled at the companions. "It's against His will!"

Her cries woke the children, who stared at her in confusion. Some started to cry.

"This is all we need," In-Su hissed. With a curse, he rushed at Ji-Su and hauled her up in his arms. She kicked and screamed at him, clawed at his face and drew bloody scratches down his chin. In-Su hustled her to the nearest house where Ha Jun rested. Woo Jin followed right on his heels. He wanted to wrestle Ji Su from In-Su's arms, but how could he fight against his eldest brother in such a manner? He watched in horror as In-Su slammed Ji Su against the

wall, knocking the air from her and silencing her. In-Su pinned her hands against the stone blocks and brought his face so close to hers that their noses almost touched.

"I cannot and will not allow you to bring ruin upon our plans with your ravings!" he bellowed at her. Ji Su, catching her breath again, shrieked. The children of the village gathered around the window, sobs spreading among them. The monk appeared at In-Su's side with a cloth, stuffed it into Ji Su's mouth, and tied it around the back of her head. Then he bound her hands behind her back while the three champions of the spirit hustled the children back towards the tunnel's mouth so that they could eat a quick breakfast.

"She'll destroy their morale," Nam-Kyu said. "We'll have to keep her separate from the others for as long as possible. She'll need to remain gagged."

The monk went into one of the pockets of his gray robes and produced a small vial. "Don't breathe this in," he warned the others. He uncorked the vial and poured a few drops through the gag. Ji Su tried not to swallow, but she had no choice. At first, she struggled, rubbing scratches against herself along the rough surface of the brick wall. Within moments, however, a glazed look stole into her eyes. Her mouth fell slack, her body limp.

"She must remain semi-conscious," he said to In-Su. "It'll be too risky to bring her with us otherwise, and we can't leave her behind. She has to reveal everything she knows to the governor. We must understand how damaging the teachings of Hana-Nim are."

Ha Jun, roused by the commotion, pushed himself

to his feet with a heavy grunt. "How can I help, elder brothers?" he asked.

"Take her." In-Su handed Ji Su to Ha Jun. "She'll ride with you. Protect her, for she must make it back to Jeju."

Woo Jin stepped forward. The sight of Ji Su being held by Ha Jun caused a sharp ache to pierce his chest. "Eldest brother," he said, his voice strained in his ears, "I have room to carry her on my horse."

The monk shot Woo Jin a look of impatience that made him wince. "Now is the time to obey, not to question," Nam-Kyu said.

The expression on In-Su's face was no kinder. "Your role is vital," he said. "Do as you've been instructed."

Woo Jin had never seen that look in In-Su's eyes before. Somewhere in that hard gaze lurked fear. But the soldier had pushed it deep down and now all that revealed itself was his desire to take care of the task at hand.

Woo Jin bowed at the command, but his eyes lingered on Ha Jun, who slung a compliant Ji Su over his shoulder. With one hand, Ha Jun picked up the sword that Kun Woo had struggled to carry. Both In-Su and Nam-Kyu's eyes widened in surprise at how effortlessly Ha Jun carried the weapon as he went outside to join the others. The two men exchanged glances, but said no more, leaving the house to prepare for the journey.

Watching Ha Jun's hands on Ji Su, his hand braced against her lower back to steady her on his shoulder, caused a hollowness to open inside of Woo Jin. A dark emotion that he could not quite name swiftly filled the emptiness. He should be the only one to touch her like that. If not him, it shouldn't be Ha Jun.

Nausea crept through him, his stomach turning and bile filling his mouth. He swallowed it down and went to the barrels they had placed near the tunnel. His hands trembled as he reached for the arrows and put them into the quiver. He wrapped string around ten and placed them beneath his pack on the horse. He left the rest loose so that he could carry them as he rode. The small pyeonjeons, he kept in their special package tucked beneath his hanbok. The poison remained secreted there, too.

Woo Jin hadn't kept track of the Dark Elf during the night and saw her now sitting cross-legged on the ground near the children. She ate her breakfast and stared north towards the Seoraksan Mountains with her blue and brown eyes. If she knew something, she didn't speak her thoughts to the companions.

The opportunity to assassinate the treacherous foreigner would probably present itself to him soon, yet Woo Jin found it difficult to focus on Windshine at this time despite the fact that his family's lives were at stake. All of his thoughts swirled around one person.

Ji Su.

He desired to be the girl's savior in this darkest moment in her life. That, and only that, was the priority that occupied his thoughts. Windshine could wait until after he'd won Ji Su's praise by saving the children of the village.

The young ones finished eating, and finally all was

prepared. The companions mounted their horses. In-Su and Kun Woo took the lead at the head of the procession of children and led them through the tunnel to the temple gates. The champions of the spirit took the rear and played a fast-paced tune to keep the young ones focused on moving as one group. The monk and Ha Jun rode to the right, and Woo Jin rode to the left. Windshine trailed behind them, her gaze ever northward, her expression unreadable.

In-Su raised the temple gates and they streamed out onto the dirt path passing through the killing fields. They paused so that Nam-Kyu could dismount. With one of his small knives, he sliced open his palm. Walking through the tall grass, he closed his hand into a fist and let droplets of blood fall on the rotting corpses of the grandfathers. When he returned to the companions, he said, "The blood creates a bridge so that the souls will know where they are needed. I can bring back fifteen and still be able to ride with you. This will require vast quantities of spiritual energy, however. I will be useless for any other kind of combat from hence further."

"How strong will the grandfathers be?" In-Su asked.

"Undead warriors are powerful," Nam-Kyu replied. "They will not tire, and they do not fear. Normal attacks will damage them, but they feel no pain. I'll be able to repair their bodies for a while, but the risk to myself for becoming their gateway back to the world of the living is great. If I lose control, the next realm will snatch my soul away as payment for my weakness."

"Brothers!" Ki Ha raised his hand to his ear. "Listen! Something is coming."

It was faint at first, but soon the sound of hooves pounding on the earth could be heard echoing across the plains. The companions and the children looked up and saw a line of North Hanguk soldiers charging toward them on horseback. Shadowy tendrils trailed behind the soldiers like ripped pieces of cloth. The northerners would momentarily disappear within folds of darkness, to reappear moments later.

In-Su turned to Ha Jun. "Lead the children towards the forests. The rest of us will take care of the soldiers."

"You want me to flee!" Ha Jun gasped out, his face reddening.

"I want you to obey," In-Su snapped. Ha Jun lowered his head, then called to the children to follow him away from the companions. Ji Su, settled behind him, began to wriggle. Her efforts were feeble, but greater life seemed to be returning to her as the North Hanguk soldiers closed in upon them.

Nam-Kyu shook his head. "The potion is wearing off too fast. It must be that meddling foreign god revitalizing her! Damn that Hana-Nim," he growled. "I don't have time to administer more to her now, I must concentrate."

"Watch her," In-Su commanded Ha Jun, who was leading the children away. Then In-Su turned to Woo Jin. "They're sure to have archers this time, so your speed must outpace theirs. The archers will stop first to attack. That's who the grandfathers will target. You're to use the reanimated dead as cover. Ride right behind them and take out as many of the soldiers as you can. Kun Woo and I will sweep in from their right flank and take out those who remain."

Woo Jin nodded. He took the reins in one hand and held five arrows between his fingers in the other. A great scream erupted from the horizon and shook the earth. Everyone froze and gazed up at the sky. The horses kicked up their front legs, their nostrils flaring, their braying wild with fear. Woo Jin could barely control his mount as terror rose within him and threatened to yank his senses under. He stared in horror at the dark morning sky, his heart banging against his chest, his breathing catching in his throat.

It can't be, he thought. *The northerners are coming to capture the girls, so they wouldn't send that, would they? That thing is for massacring. It's for destroying. It's death from above on leather wings!*

There was no mistaking the creature as it soared through the air towards them. A dragon, called up from the blackest nightmares and racing towards them at startling speeds.

"Woo Jin!" In-Su yelled above the dragon's scream. Desperation twisted his haggard face as his eyes darted from the dragon, to the children, to Woo Jin, and back to the dragon again. "Its weakness is between the scales. Aim there and you might have a chance!"

In-Su spun to the champions of the spirit. "Direct all of your music upon him! He's our only hope!"

Woo Jin tried to squeeze breath out of his constricted lungs and failed. A great pressure built up in his forehead and threatened to burst through his skull.

His eldest brother's command was madness. In-Su was ordering him to face a dragon, alone? Woo Jin could barely control his horse, which kicked in an effort throw him from its back. Yet he was to challenge a dragon?

He couldn't do this. He *wouldn't* do this. Not now, not after he'd found Ji Su and had a reason to live.

Run! He must grab Ji Su from Ha Jun and escape. No one else mattered, nothing else mattered, except survival.

Ki Ha raised the percussion high over his head and slammed it against the taunt drum skin. A thunderous sound roared out at Woo Jin, slammed into him, and buried his terror under reckless abandon. All of his apprehensions were crushed down deep inside of himself to be replaced with carefree overconfidence. The power of Ki Ha's successive beats upon the drum pummeled Woo Jin's emotions into electrifying exuberance. Woo Jin laughed, his body shaking as the part of him that feared struggled against the music but lost to the rhythm of the drumming.

With a wild cry, Woo Jin spurred his horse forward, his heart racing at speeds that left him lightheaded. Clenching onto the steed with his legs, he released the reins. With a steady hand, he nocked an arrow. He didn't stop laughing with mad glee as he charged the dragon.

The dragon roared. A scale shifted under the beast's chest as it pumped its wide leathery wings. Woo Jin, with perfect timing, released the arrow, and it hit true, lodging itself into the dragon's flesh exposed between its scales. The beast's wounded shriek was like a blow all its own, and for a moment Woo Jin heard little else. He clutched at his head in pain, temporary freed from the spell of the music. Terror swallowed his false confidence as the dragon lurched up into the sky, a shower of hot blood raining down upon Woo Jin.

Seeing the perfect strike of the arrow, Woo Jin whooped with joy despite the pain of his ears. He had done it! He alone had slain a dragon with a single shot! Truly, he would be called a hero!

The dragon, however, didn't fall dead from the sky. It continued to shriek, but a mad rage filled its earth-shaking cries. Woo Jin watched in fascinated horror as the beast opened its fanged maw to reveal a long serpent tongue. Something in the back of its throat flashed, and a massive ball of fire exploded from its mouth and slammed into the forests the children had been racing towards. The trees burst into flame.

Woo Jin saw In-Su screaming something. From the rounded shape of his lips, it looked like he was screaming *No!*, repeatedly. The children gazed at the flying monster in dumb fear, their mouths dropped open, their eyes wide and shining with tears. Escape through the forest was impossible now, and the dragon circled back in their direction.

In-Su and Kun Woo raced to the children of Goseong, pushing their horses at a relentless gallop, their swords drawn. The dragon soared above the earth to pierce the sky. Then it folded its wings along its sides and dropped from the air with such force that Woo Jin thought it would slam into the ground. At the last moment, it spread its wings to lurch back up into the sky, but not before it snatched In-Su in its claws. Its long talons pierced In-Su's chest and stomach in multiple places as it ripped the soldier off of his horse.

"Elder brother!" Woo Jin cried out. He spurned his horse forward, but the dragon returned to the sky. It shoved the struggling In-Su into the jagged fangs of his mouth and chewed, shredding In-Su into fleshy chunks of meat.

"Woo Jin!" The monk yelled. "It's too late for him, but you still have a mission to do. Don't forget the quest!"

Woo Jin pulled hard on the reins of the horse and turned to the monk still in the fields at the entrance of the temple.

"What am I supposed to do?" Woo Jin shouted back at him. "How am I supposed to kill the dragon?"

An arrow whizzed past his head. Woo Jin spun around and cursed. The North Hanguk soldiers had reached them. Their archers fired from the back of their horses as they closed in upon the companions.

Nam-Kyu, face resigned, grabbed all the knives hanging from his belt and tossed them up into the air. "I'll give you everything I have!"

The monk clasped the golden three-legged crow medallion and chanted in tongues that rose in frequency. The tones overlapped each other, though only the monk spoke, and they deepened and seemed to drift off to corners of space just beyond reality. The knives spun in the air, paused as one, then darted down and slammed into Nam-Kyu, embedding themselves into his body. Woo Jin screamed, but the monk did not stop chanting. The knives kept moving, the blades carving into him and spraying his blood upon the rotting corpses of the killing fields.

The monk abruptly fell silent. He gazed at Woo Jin and smiled through the blood leaking down his splattered face. Then he collapsed into the dirt and stirred no more.

Woo Jin began to dismount when, around him, the bodies of the grandfathers and brothers of Goseong rose from the tall grass. At least three dozen pushed themselves up from the ground and opened their mouths to release agonized howls that drove Woo Jin's horse mad with fright. He struggled to control it as the undead turned their eyes glowing with a harsh light upon him. Their bodies did not reform as the monk had said they would, and ragged pieces of flesh hung from their bones.

Their condition didn't seem to affect them. They turned their rotting forms to the North Hanguk soldiers and, as one, dashed forward with supernatural speed, attacking.

Woo Jin tried to urge his horse to follow the undead villagers, but the dragon's shriek made him turn once more to the burning forests. The dragon had consumed In-Su, the soldier's blood smeared across its scaly lips. It glided upon currents above them, its orange eyes focused on the children of Goseong. Hunger shone through its murderous gaze. A plume of smoke snaked up from the beast's nostrils. The dragon opened its maw and inhaled.

Woo Jin nocked an arrow and kicked the horse in the flanks. It leapt forward towards the dragon. To his left, he saw the three champions of the spirit and Kun Woo racing their steeds in the same direction. Still they played. Woo Jin opened himself to the melodies, and the music speared through him. Doubt, fear, indecision; the magic in the champions of the spirits' enchanting songs buried those emotions.

Closer, Woo Jin thought, his horse shuddering under the strain of the relentless gallop, *just a little closer!* He pulled back the bowstring, his arms steady as he calculated the distance between himself and the dragon. The dragon seemed to have learned its lesson and kept out of arrow range. Woo Jin pushed the horse faster, but he simply couldn't reach the beast in time. The dragon inhaled, the plumes of smoke snaking from its nostrils whooshing down its long throat. With a roar, it breathed out a cyclone of fire that spread out in wide flaming tongues over the wide-eyed, immobile children.

Woo Jin released the arrow, but it was futile. The dragon flew too high up, and Woo Jin was too late to save the children of Goseong from the engulfing flames.

16

Whimpers escaped the quivering lips of the cowering children of Goseong. The cyclone of dragon's breath cascaded down upon them in bright tongues of orange flame that set aglow the sweat glistening on the young ones' faces. Tears of frustration flowed from Woo Jin's eyes, the instant freezing in time. He watched the flames undulate in the air like water above the terrified expressions on the children's faces. Each detail of their horror seared its way into his mind, and he realized he wouldn't forget the grotesque vision for the rest of his life.

Then time whipped forward, and the dragon's breath flowed to the ground in relentless waves.

Elvish words cut through the dragon's roar. A white and blue cloth shot forward, spread above the children's heads, widened to shield all of them, and caught the flames in its fabric. Here and there, holes burned through, and the agonized screams of several children pierced the air as the dragon's breath dripped onto them. The flattened cloth saved most of them, however, and Woo Jin turned to see Windshine speaking her strange language, the hem of her robes stretching from her to incredible proportions and protecting the children from the dragon's attack.

Ha Jun rode near her. He ripped the gag from Ji Su's mouth, freed her hands, and lifted her down to the ground. She dashed to the children who smoldered beneath the places where the fabric had burned through, that western symbol bouncing against her chest with each stride.

The dragon shrieked its rage. Its serpent head swiveled to Ji Su. Woo Jin watched in horror as the beast swooped down upon her. He kicked his horse forward, the brothers of the champions of the spirt and the soldier, Kun Woo, flanking his right and left. Woo Jin nocked another arrow, pulled the bowstring back, and released it. His shot was perfect, but the dragon scales slid over the exposed flesh he was aiming for as its muscles shifted. The arrow bounced against the beast's bright scales.

Woo Jin readied another arrow, but before he could release it, Ha Jun leapt from his horse to the ground to stand in front of Ji Su. He raised his two-handed sword and shouted a word in elvish. He swung the sword and a massive gale of wind struck the dragon and sent it tumbling up into the sky.

Ji Su reached the afflicted children, but she was too late. Those that had been caught in the dragon breath had burned away to bone and ash, and she fell to her knees, sobbing.

"We don't have time for this," Ha Jun yelled at her. "The dragon will return!"

Woo Jin stiffened at Ha Jun's harsh words. The sounds of battle behind him drifted closer. He turned to see the undead of Goseong had wiped out half of the North Hanguk soldiers. With their hands and teeth, they relentlessly attacked the soldiers who hacked away at them. The northerners were being torn apart, but did not retreat, pushing forward despite their mounting casualties.

Behind Woo Jin, Ji Su screamed. He looked back and saw the battle had caught her attention. Regaining her feet, she ran at the melee and shouted, "Hana-Nim! Take the souls of our kinsmen back to your paradise!"

A bright, pale light erupted from the symbol around her neck. It splintered into dozens of shafts and pierced the rotting corpses of the grandfathers and brothers of the village. The undead stopped gouging, clawing, and chewing on the North Hanguk warriors. They lifted their heads as one up to the blue sky. Peaceful sighs spread between them, and from their lips they uttered a grateful, "*Ah Men.*"

The grandfathers and brothers peeled off from the northern men and fell, lifeless, to the ground. Woo Jin stared in disbelief, unable to move as the soldiers hacked away at the corpses with cries of relief and victory.

"The fool!" Jae Jin gasped. "She's doomed us."

"Maybe not," Kun Woo said, and kicked his horse

into a gallop towards the Dark Elf. "Help us fight," he shouted at her, "and we may win."

With a gesture of her hand, Windshine withdrew the cloth spread out over the children's heads. It shrank back to her, wrapping itself into the hem of her robe once more.

"I broke my vow to the Emperor out of pity," she said, "but that will be the only time. Companions of South Hanguk!" The brown in the blue of her eyes swirled like desert sands caught in a maelstrom. "*Save yourselves!*"

The dragon's shriek of anger mirrored the rage building within Woo Jin as he gazed at the Dark Elf. Images of In-Su, impaled and consumed, flashed in his vision. He thought of the monk, Nam-Kyu, nobly sacrificing himself to give the children of Goseong a chance to escape. He then cast his eyes to Ji Su, his love. But because of the foreign religion, she had foolishly taken away the very chance for survival his elder brothers had given them by calling away the souls of the dead.

As if she could feel his gaze, Ji Su turned to him. For a moment their eyes locked. Then she spun to Ha Jun and asked, "Can you stop the dragon with that sword? Can you protect the children of Goseong?"

The rage inside of Woo Jin flared into hatred. What right did Ha Jun have to use that elvish sword to save the people of South Hanguk? If Ha Jun became a hero, who would his loyalties belong to?

The puzzle pieces clicked into place. The governors of the provinces of South Hanguk were all heroes. The dark elves had been traveling with companions on quests for generations. What influences had they had on the outcome of the quests? When good men like In-Su and Nam-Kyu, willing to risk it all, died, that left traitors like Ha Jun, who attained victory with the help of foreign objects.

At last, Woo Jin grasped why the government official had commissioned him to assassinate the Dark Elf. The foreign spread had to be stopped in the country of South Hanguk. Woo Jin had been gifted the very means to do so now.

The pyeonjeons.

"Woo Jin!" Kun Woo called to him. "Ride with me."

Kun Woo turned to the champions of the spirit. "Bring up the rear. We have to attack the northerners before they realize the undead are no more."

The three brothers readied their instruments. Jae Jin placed the long flute to his lips and blew a melody that sank into Woo Jin and gave his actions grace. The deep beats from Ki Ha's drum amplified his confidence, and the sharp stringed notes from Jae Ho's lute quickened his movements.

Alongside Kun Woo, Woo Jin spurred his horse forward. This time, however, the music didn't place him completely under its control. The burning hatred, the need to liberate South Hanguk from the clutches of foreign influences, cordoned off a piece of himself determined to kill Windshine. His chance had finally come.

He broke off from Kun Woo and rode at a wide left angle along the flank of the North Hanguk soldiers. They were finally redirecting their attention away from the corpses they had been butchering. Above his head, the dragon roared, its dark shadow scarring the land as it circled overhead. Woo Jin could do nothing about the beast until it came closer, so he focused on what was in front of him. He aimed and released the bowstring, striking a soldier down. He fired another arrow, then another. With three down, the soldiers turned to him. Those with bows fired back, their arrows whizzing past his head. Woo Jin's aim was surer.

To the northerners' right, Kun Woo attacked.

Now the North Hanguk soldiers' focus split. Woo Jin took them out from one side and Kun Woo cut them down from the other. A tenth soldier fell, then an eleventh. Only some two dozen remained. One soldier wielding a long spear launched the weapon at Woo Jin just as Kun Woo's sword sliced through the back of the northerner's neck. The spear sped true and struck Woo Jin's horse through its gaping mouth, splitting the animal's skull in two.

The horse violently jerked, and Woo Jin flew from its back. He tucked his body around the bow to protect it as he hit the ground hard with his right shoulder. He rolled to avoid the horse flipping over him, its back legs barely missing him. The animal slid across the grass to come to a sudden stop in the dirt behind him. Woo Jin regained his feet and searched for his arrows that had scattered from the quiver.

"Kun Woo is outnumbered," Ki Ha shouted as the three brothers rode past Woo Jin. For the first time, they stopped playing and slid their swords from their sheaths as they charged into the remaining North Hanguk soldiers to aid their elder brother.

Woo Jin was alone. The chance he had been waiting for arrived. He turned to look across the field and saw Ha Jun standing in front of Ji Su and the children of Goseong, his sword raised. All of them cast their eyes up at the dragon overhead. The beast had not attacked again, its gaze fixed on the elvish sword Ha Jun wielded.

Woo Jin crawled back to his dead horse, searched along his scattered belongings and found the special bow Official Yeo had given him in the wooden pavilion on Jeju. He reached into his hanbok, removed five of the pyeonjeons and the vial of poison, and coated the tips with the dark liquid. The Dark Elf was on her horse staring at the children huddled near her.

If the dragon attacked, would she protect herself but let the rest of children burn if the companions could not save them? Woo Jin clenched his teeth as he prepared an arrow, his hands steady. He aimed and released the bowstring in a single motion. The arrow ripped forward with a shrill whistle and struck Windshine in the chest, passing through her with the incredible force of its momentum. The Dark Elf issued a short scream and collapsed from her horse, landing at the feet of the children of South Hanguk.

It was over.

The children screamed, and Ji Su and Ha Jun turned to see what disturbed them. The dragon roared in triumph. It opened its massive maw, the spark in the back of its throat ignited, and once again, a cyclone of fire erupted from the back of its throat towards the children. Ha Jun spun to the oncoming dragon's breath, shouted a word of elvish, and swung his sword. A wall of water erupted from the blade and slammed into the fire. A cloudburst of steam filled the air, and the dragon shrieked as its flames evaporated before finding their mark.

Woo Jin prepared another pyeonjeon, aimed up at the distracted dragon, and let loose the arrow at its underbelly as the scales shifted to expose the flesh underneath. The small arrow struck true and buried itself into the beast, disappearing inside its flesh. The dragon's pained screams rumbled the earth. Woo Jin prepared another arrow, but paused as, out of the corner of his eye, he saw Ji Su race towards the children and drop down to her knees at Windshine's side.

No!

He leveled the arrow at her and aimed. His hands trembled as he released the bowstring. The arrow shot forward with a high-pitched whistle but zipped past Ji Su's head, missing. The dragon reared its head towards the shrilling sound as it floundered in the sky, its blood spilling from the deep wound and splattering the ground. With a powerful beat of its wings, it soared into the air. Woo Jin prepared another arrow as the dragon dove at him. He didn't flinch as its maw opened to reveal jagged teeth. He let loose the arrow, which pierced the dragon's upper mouth and exited out the back of its head.

The dragon screamed and folded its wings as it slammed into Woo Jin, crushing him.

17

Woo Jin knew he could not stay.

Beneath the massive bulk of the dead dragon, he bled out into the earth of South Hanguk. This was his land, and to it his body would return. He would always be a part of this country.

That essential spark which was Woo Jin existed outside of his physical casing now. Around him, the living world grew faint, the colors fading to gray, the sounds quieting to silence, the smells dissipating into the ether. Even as the other reality beckoned him, Woo Jin marveled at his accomplishment. Alone, he had slain a dragon. He had saved the children of Goseong. They would sing his praise one day. They would remember his name.

Snatches of conversation from a faraway place floated to Woo Jin. He listened and recognized the voices of his great grandparents. They had died when he was a child, yet he still recognized the way they sounded. Somewhere in the beyond, his ancestors waited for him, summoning him to his clan. He must join them in whatever struggles and conflicts the next life presented. He didn't know if he was prepared, but the choice was not his to make. His time amongst the living had slipped away to nothing.

One more moment, he asked of death. He wanted to see how the story of the village of children ended. He peered into the living world through the growing haze swallowing the senses he'd known since birth. Through the shifting shadows, he saw the remaining North Hanguk soldiers retreating. The three champions of the spirit played a song of triumph as Kun Woo chased after the northerners, cutting down all he could catch. With the dragon dead, nothing stood in the way of the children of Goseong escaping the borderlands.

The quest had ended a success.

Woo Jin gazed across the fields, but someone blocked his sight. The figure took shape, and he saw the Dark Elf sharing this reality with him. Her form wavered like smoke, and she stared at him with those brown and blue eyes. He returned her gaze and saw neither reproach nor forgiveness in her expression. Then a pale light enveloped her, and she disappeared. Farther away, Woo Jin saw Ji Su praying over the Dark Elf. Windshine stirred and lifted her head.

Woo Jin sighed.

Finally, he turned to Ha Jun. He memorized every detail of the hostler's face and imagined what he would look like as he aged. In whatever new reality Woo Jin would soon enter, he promised to keep an eye on the hostler. If Ha Jun became corrupted by the foreigner, if he betrayed his country, Woo Jin would exert all the powers he could muster from this next life to stop him, for Woo Jin could now see the truth.

There will be one, and it would be Ha Jun who became a great hero and influence the course of South Hanguk's history.

The End

ABOUT TODD SULLIVAN

Todd Sullivan teaches English as a Second Language, and English Literature & Writing in Asia. He has had numerous short stories, novelettes, and novellas published across several countries, including Thailand, the U.K., Australia, the U.S., and Canada. He is a practitioner of the sword-fighting martial arts, kumdo/kendo, and has trained in fencing (foil), Muay Thai, Capoeira, Wing Chun, and JKD. He graduated from Queens College with a Master of Fine Arts in Creative Writing and received a Bachelor of Arts in English from Georgia State University. He attended the Bread Loaf Writers' Conference and the National Book Foundation Summer Writing Camps. He currently lives in Taipei, Taiwan, and looks forward to studying Mandarin.

www.ingramcontent.com/pod-product-compliance
Lightning Source LLC
Chambersburg PA
CBHW051841170626
46807CB00003B/1297